MISSION
CATASTROPHE

Mini Adventures

Edited By Lynsey Evans

First published in Great Britain in 2024 by:

Young Writers
Remus House
Coltsfoot Drive
Peterborough
PE2 9BF
Telephone: 01733 890066
Website: www.youngwriters.co.uk

FOREWORD

Young Writers was created in 1991 with the express purpose of promoting and encouraging creative writing. Each competition we create is tailored to the relevant age group, hopefully giving each student the inspiration and incentive to create their own piece of work, whether it's a poem or a short story. We truly believe that seeing their work in print gives students a sense of achievement and pride in their work and themselves.

Mission Catastrophe gave secondary students the opportunity to write about disasters, ranging from world-ending natural events and the consequences of war, to day-to-day mishaps and minor setbacks. These students have explored the consequences of catastrophe big and small, resulting in a varied and entertaining collection of stories.

One of the biggest challenges, aside from facing floods, avoiding avalanches and dealing with lost phones, was to create a mini saga with a beginning, middle and end! Writing with a word constraint allows students to focus on vocabulary choice and takes away the fear of long-form writing, ensuring they get straight to the heart of the story.

The thrilling stories in this collection are sure to set your pulses racing and we're sure you'll agree that Mission Catastrophe has been a success!

CONTENTS

Broughton Hall Catholic High School, Liverpool

Connie McGowan (12)   1

Kingsbury High School, Kingsbury

Heer Shah (13)   2
Sinai Ansah (14)   3
Hong-Yin Ma (13)   4
Panav Panchani (13)   5
Ayan Patel (12)   6
Daniel Kamyab (14)   7
Amir Dehvari (13)   8
Paula Jimson (12)   9
Noemi Tibu (13)   10
Ianis Paduraru (14)   11
Mayan Bhavan (11)   12
Aadya Jha (11)   13
Golnar Eshaghtabar Andvari (12)   14
Athith Mohanathasan (12)   15

St Boniface's Catholic College, Plymouth

Tyler Goddard (13)   16
Zachary Watts (12)   17
Mateusz Janek (12)   18
Rui Quiterio (12)   19
Adrian Koziak (13)   20
Ewan Bennett (13)   21
Jacob Brewer (13)   22
Jack Greenhouse (13)   23
Kaif Ahmed (13)   24
Jack Bailey (12)   25
Finn Hawking (13)   26

Harvey McGrath (13)   27
Jack Morton (14)   28
Seth Hawker (12)   29
Jesudunsin Shoyemi (12)   30
Adeniran Praise Oluwadarasimi (11)   31
Riley Coombe (13)   32
Lucas Kaminski (13)   33
Fletcher Newman (12)   34
Reagan Andrew (13)   35
David Makar (11)   36
Jack Harris (12)   37
Rocco Stronach (13)   38
Max Ball (12)   39

The Gatwick School, Crawley

Faheem Kamara (11)   40
Ewan Watson (12)   41
Angel Aiken (12)   42
Aisha Khan (13)   43
Aimel Arif (12)   44
Sydney Kazimierczak-Morfoot (13)   45
Sumanohara Sai Sri Mallipudi (12)   46
Sophie Hemmant (11)   47
Jacob Byrne (12)   48
Amy Hussey (11)   49
Eliza Zorgji (12)   50
Josh Parekh (12)   51
Isabella Stagg (11)   52
Skyla Allerton-Hilton (12)   53
Niamh Collins (12)   54

The Moulton School & Science College, Moulton

Jaxson Shakir (13)	55

The Phoenix Collegiate, West Bromwich

Jake Smith (14)	56
Kelsey Bushell (14)	57
Charlie Walden (13)	58
Melissa Diggins (14)	59

Tunbridge Wells Grammar School for Boys, Tunbridge Wells

Jorge William Martin (11)	60
Jenson Tatton	61
Edward Oliver (13)	62
James Jaswal (12)	63
Raff Curtis (13)	64
Ethan Tran (11)	65
David Efimov (13)	66
Thomas Garcia (13)	67
Rory White	68
Dexter Howie (12)	69
Oscar Brooks-Wilkins (13)	70
Orlando Clement (13)	71
Aadam Chatha (13)	72
Lewis Hook (13)	73
Oliver Clark (11)	74
James Burdis (13)	75
Joseph Tyler (12)	76
Alex Martin (13)	77
William Underwood (13)	78
Rupert Walton (11)	79
Max Frith (12)	80
Matthew Drane (13)	81
Tom Binks (14)	82
Oscar White (13)	83
Zachary Bonval (13)	84
Finlay Heffernan (12)	85
Louis Dennis (12)	86
George Cunningham (14)	87

Luke Williams (13)	88
Marco Mellinger (13)	89
Sebastian White (14)	90
Orhan Imad Murad (11)	91
Tom Moriaty-Cole (12)	92
Edward Nunn (12)	93
Hadrien Mauduit (11)	94
George Hale (12)	95
Taylor Jones (12)	96
Noah White (12)	97
Fred Kolbe (12)	98
Leo Seadon (12)	99
Samuel Chamberlain (12)	100
Connor Fairless (12)	101
Leo Heathcoat (12)	102
Luca Woolger (12)	103
Harry Mauldon (12)	104
Benjamin Wackett (13)	105
Leo Thomas (13)	106
Jacob Ashlee (13)	107
Jamie Bothwell (13)	108
Aleksander Hajdukovic (12)	109
Caleb Jackson (11)	110
Louie Groves (11)	111
Luca Bonval (11)	112
Samuel Philpott (12)	113
Alfie Elliott (12)	114
Alastair Brunning (11)	115
Ethan Byrne (12)	116
Mark French	117
Charlie Adams (12)	118
Maxwell Carter (12)	119
Tyus Wiltshire (12)	120
Sebastian Jiggins (12)	121
Charlie Blaker (12)	122
Freddie Gipp (13)	123
Ethan Tsui (12)	124
Arthur Magoola (13)	125
George Sillett (12)	126
Billy Allcorn (12)	127
Harry King (11)	128
Maren Grover (12)	129
Javier Oliver Torrijos (13)	130

Yuvraj Singh (12)	131	Pranav Gurram (13)	174
Zakarya Haouani (12)	132	Dexter Carroll (11)	175
Oscar Du Toit (12)	133	Aditya Kampani (12)	176
Danny Germer (13)	134	Joel Philpott (12)	177
Andrew Macleod (12)	135	Hudson Holland-Keefe (12)	178
Olly Brown (14)	136	Jygraj Khamba (12)	179
Albert Edwards (12)	137	Stanley Bonas (13)	180
Ruairi Brennan (12)	138	Oliver Barker (13)	181
Etienne Saunders (14)	139	James Bennett (12)	182
Thomas Sweeney (12)	140	Stanley Grayland (12)	183
Alex Stockton (13)	141	Daniel Soanes (12)	184
Will Steer (12)	142	Toby Portlock (13)	185
Isaac de Ruiter (11)	143	Balthazar Gyring-Nielsen (12)	186
Lewis Ketterer (12)	144	Dylan Gregan-Salvado (12)	187
Mackenzie Garstang (13)	145	Sebastian Higham (12)	188
Will Clarke (13)	146	Andrew Champkin (14)	189
Szymon Pelczynski (14)	147	Nikita Hubin (12)	190
Bill Chesworth (12)	148	Younus Baig (12)	191
Hezekiah Cuthbert (11)	149	Theo Slade (12)	192
Xander Lonie (12)	150	John Davies (12)	193
Olly Brooks (12)	151	James Wong (12)	194
Oliver Swann (12)	152		
Leon Williams (12)	153		
Tommy Sands (12)	154		
Stefan Van Der Merwe (12)	155		
Hassan Elzaafarany (13)	156		
Jack Wetz (12)	157		
Arthur Mountain (11)	158		
Sam Saunders (13)	159		
Blake Barlow (11)	160		
Johnny Verrechia (12)	161		
Shea O'Hagan (11)	162		
Jack Randall (12)	163		
Alex McGourty (12)	164		
Jack Bennett (12)	165		
Clarke Henry (11)	166		
Seth Cockfield (12)	167		
Abdelrahman Elzaafarany (13)	168		
Luca Smith (13)	169		
Harry Mucklow (12)	170		
Lewis Hayter (12)	171		
Owen Garner (11)	172		
Joseph Johnson (12)	173		

THE MINI SAGAS

Mission Catastrophe

In a cruel world of shattered dreams, a heart once full of hope, now filled with deplorable sorrow. A love once vibrant now faded like a distant memory. Echoes of laughter ominously replaced by the haunting silence of loss. Protracted regret filled the frigid air, suffocating chance of redemption. Dark consumed the past bright spirit, leaving only a hollow shell behind. Cries of despair emerged from quivering lips, irises now red and drenched with hot, salty tears. In the depths of depression, a tragic tale unfolding, reminding one of the fragile nature of the excruciating pain of unfulfilled dreams.

Connie McGowan (12)
Broughton Hall Catholic High School, Liverpool

Untitled

Regret! I had just reached the shutters. My 'friends' locked me out. The loud silence was heard. I stood there, realising what happened. The thick smoke was choking me. That's when I saw those peculiar glowing eyes. I couldn't see anything apart from them. Haunting me.

Regret grew upon me. Why'd I decide to do this? I remembered. There was an emergency exit on the other side. Without thinking, I ran. The glowing eyes seemed to be chasing me.

Suddenly, I tripped. 'It' surrounded me from every direction. Growling and screeching sounds closed up towards me. Someone shot a bullet.

Heer Shah (13)
Kingsbury High School, Kingsbury

The End

I didn't stop. I didn't even look back. The rumbling was enough to throw me off earth. Trees bowed their heads while flamboyant flames invasively zigzagged among them. Every lifeform was driven to the edge of the world.
How did this happen? There was only one simple answer. Humans. A sinuous fox careered before me as its little legs manoeuvred a perilous escape. Here came altruistic Mother Nature who gave us her all. This was her penultimate warning. It was finally time for Mother Nature to deliver her austere punishment for humanity's abhorrent crimes.
Then I took my final breath.

Sinai Ansah (14)
Kingsbury High School, Kingsbury

Homework Disaster

In a rush to submit the assignment, you darted through the chaotic streets, the weight of your homework heavy in your hands.

Suddenly, a gust of wind snatched the paper from your grasp, sending it swirling into the air like a lost leaf. Panic surged as you chased after it, but to no avail. The paper danced out of reach, disappearing into the bustling cityscape. With dread sinking in, you realised the catastrophic truth: your homework was gone, lost amidst the urban chaos.

Frantic apologies and desperate searches followed but the irreversible damage was done, leaving you to face consequences.

Hong-Yin Ma (13)
Kingsbury High School, Kingsbury

Vortex Of Death

Nolan sat at the back of the antique geography class, bored. He felt like bunking off but knew his mum wouldn't be happy. As he stared out the window, he noticed the clouds started turning as black as the night sky.
Suddenly, he saw something he didn't even think was real. A tornado. "Run!" he roared.
Instantly, everyone packed their belongings and started running for their lives, literally. The whole school erupted and Nolan rushed out the school gates. Everyone else ran to safety, but Nolan only had one choice, ahead, as the swirling vortex of death blared behind him.

Panav Panchani (13)
Kingsbury High School, Kingsbury

The End Is Near

The sirens rang as the chaos flooded the streets. Panic burst as the thick smoke of darkness choked us all. Gunshots were heard in the distance as bodies flew past me. A broken TV lay on the floor repeating, "Breaking news, the prime minister has declared there are no laws."
The sound of tanks and bullets got closer, and so did my fear. I ran into a nearby shop, jumping over the countertop. There were two other people there. An awkward silence filled the room but then a helicopter came down, breaking the silence. They shouted, "Are there any survivors?"

Ayan Patel (12)
Kingsbury High School, Kingsbury

Rich Man's Show

Huddled around the glowing, warming fire, we recalled our memories of how it all came to play. An ordinary day, the sleepless city illuminated with the sparks of society, soon encased in horror. TVs flashed with the filthy words of the governors in their secure, cosy mansions, 'a virus'?
It had been two years since the city was tossed into a panic. Fires had lit up the infested sky since that day. Waves of the past residents turned 'rogue', masked in a Netflix fantasy. A broadcast shown in cities worldwide. We were in a rich man's show.

Daniel Kamyab (14)
Kingsbury High School, Kingsbury

The Deadly Shower

Alex hurried across the flame-filled street. The sky filled with large asteroids - seemingly endless, destroying everything. The city indeed was in ruin.

Alex felt the lump in his throat grow. His final hope was a voice in the distance crying for help. Alex dodged flying debris and fire.

Alex arrived at a ruined car park. His eyes locked onto a man banging on his car window - he was trapped! As Alex pulled on the door a large shadow covered him and the area, and as Alex looked up... he could see an asteroid falling from above... about to crush him...

Amir Dehvari (13)
Kingsbury High School, Kingsbury

Where Am I?

I didn't mean for this to happen. There was no way I was going back. The thick smoke was strangling my throat. I trekked down the narrow road in dismay. How could I be so foolish to enter that portal? I was stuck here forever in a century I hadn't been in before.

Bang! A mysterious purple aroma rose from the destroyed ground. I could hear it calling my name and I walked forward confidently. I was going back! I entered it and everything went dark.

I woke up. Where was I? I had just realised, I was in a different century.

Paula Jimson (12)
Kingsbury High School, Kingsbury

Invisible Bullet

My mind was full of worried thoughts. What would Coach say?
Bing! The button was heard. We landed. The door shot open. One by one, we walked out. As I saw what awaited us, I gasped. Armed men surrounded us as a bus waited for us in the distance.
Suddenly the captain of the team fell down as soon as she reached the bus. Like dominoes, they fell after her. The army men looked around, confused as no one touched their triggers.
I realised what was happening and tried to run back inside but it was too late. Everything went dark...

Noemi Tibu (13)
Kingsbury High School, Kingsbury

Distant Split

The outlandish air that engulfed me had frozen with time as the green giant split in two. My arm hair rose awake and every nerve jolted. I could feel my heart fluctuate with fear. When I regained my thoughts I realised every human was dead. Every cell and atom was erased from existence. The restless planet flew past the black sky while everything else was still. I was alone on the ISS and was the last ever mammal that Mother Nature created and it was the loneliest feeling ever.

It was silent until I heard the most sudden thud ever.

Ianis Paduraru (14)
Kingsbury High School, Kingsbury

Death Upon Us

The world had turned upside down from 30 degrees to the most unimaginable tsunami recorded in the world. Today could possibly be the last day of humankind as the news said that this tsunami was 500 metres tall and would wipe the entire world out in a day.

Two hours later, the tsunami was in the UK. It was about to hit my village at any time. This could be it. My last time to live my life before I died. It would be my last words before I was going to die from the tsunami.

Swim to the light.

Mayan Bhavan (11)
Kingsbury High School, Kingsbury

The Friendly Monkeys

The last thing I remembered was a dolphin and a big splash. Then I found myself on an island. I saw a monkey, waking me up then vanishing away with a big strong light.
I went deeper in the island and I saw more monkeys!
Two years passed. I knew all the monkeys now. I liked playing with them.
One day, a sudden light shone, reminding me of the past. It trapped me and all the monkeys took their masks off and turned out to be aliens! The UFO sprinted past, towards a far unknown planet.

Aadya Jha (11)
Kingsbury High School, Kingsbury

Untitled

Am I the only one left? Everyone is dead. I gasp for air and slowly drift into the abyss. My vision goes blank and I fall on the floor.

"Celeste! Something is going on!" I turn on the television and see the news. The reporter tells everyone to 'count your last breaths and goodbyes'.

I gasp in fear and run out the house to the fields. I walk through the patches of grass. The more I do, the more familiar it gets. The air thickens.

I fall. Am I the only one left?

Golnar Eshaghtabar Andvari (12)
Kingsbury High School, Kingsbury

The Ailment

The school bell rang and I dashed out as quick as lightning to go home. A new game had come out and we heard it was the most intriguing game ever.

As we played esctatically, sudden news appeared on the screen. A boy named Timmy created a virus in the forest that was spreading rapidly and would wipe out humanity in one hour. My image unexpectedly appeared on the screen saying I needed to fix this as my ancestors once had.

Would I save the planet or would I be to blame?

Athith Mohanathasan (12)
Kingsbury High School, Kingsbury

Hell's Gates Awakened

The sun beamed at the new Earth. What once was a baby blue sky, now a bloody crimson. Grassy fields reduced to crumbled dirt and trampled flowers. Where rabbits ran, corpses rattled. Every mile of beautiful Earth contrasted to Hell's new playground.

Not many remained, humanity's last horde hid away in a futile attempt of life, peeking through shadows, praying the creatures and monstrosities of Hell were to return back home. Four gruesome days were all that were needed for eight billion people to be turned to ash and a whole planet to be conquered. Our home, no longer ours.

Tyler Goddard (13)
St Boniface's Catholic College, Plymouth

The Great Greek War

Zeus gave us lightning. Poseidon gave us the ocean. Athena gave us wisdom. Aphrodite gave us love. Hephaestus gave us crafts. Ares gave us war. It all started when Prometheus gave mortals fire.

Zeus was humiliated and then the great war began between the demigods, the mortals and the Olympians.

I'm a demigod son of Hades. The war is still happening and I'm still fighting, still keeping up with the gods. I dive from bush to bush as the trees glare at me.

Then the news breaks - Zeus has been defeated. The war eventually takes me to kneeling in front of Hades.

Zachary Watts (12)
St Boniface's Catholic College, Plymouth

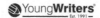
The Dark Murder

The lights went out. My first thought was an earthquake, but there was no rumbling. Quickly, I looked out my window only to see car lights flashing. My ears couldn't bear it.
I tried turning my TV on... but it wouldn't. Immediately, I thought of a power outage. "Aah! Help!"
My heart started to race... I tiptoed out of my front door, more screaming. It came from every direction. I ran back inside. I thought I was hallucinating. Blood splashed all over my window.
I ran upstairs, hoping to keep my mind off of it. I heard my front door open...

Mateusz Janek (12)
St Boniface's Catholic College, Plymouth

The Flood

After having such a boring day at the shops, I glanced over the cobbled pier and noticed the violent navy blue ocean rapidly rising! Abruptly, the ferocious waters rose to ankle height and then up to my knees...

I rushed to the car but there was no time. Swarms of thousands of people were rushing to hills, buildings and trees. However, there wasn't room for everyone to survive. As I sprinted to a nearby building (bumping into many people), I finally entered the building and pelted up the stairs to the roof. There was nothing stopping it. We were devoured.

Rui Quiterio (12)
St Boniface's Catholic College, Plymouth

The Great Gourdice

Sirens were going off. Everyone that I knew, including me, was getting rounded up and huddled together like a rope was surrounding us, getting tighter. The army told us to get in the silent trucks. The bombers and fighters whistled by and we were just waiting for a bomb to hit us, yet one never did.

Gourdice was a storm of bullets, shells and debris and we needed to somehow navigate it. We heard huge booms and crashes. The truck was coated in some camo, including leaves, and some noise protection device covered the engine.

Suddenly we heard a whistle above...

Adrian Koziak (13)
St Boniface's Catholic College, Plymouth

The Night The World Ended

It was calm, the world beneath my feet; I thought I could do anything but I could have never expected what these events would lead to, a blast, a plume of smoke and darkness.
I awoke, my lungs burning. It was a hellish nightmare place and I was a solitary soul among the dirt and rubble.
Suddenly, I heard it, a loud robotic voice. It echoed over the wasteland and my instincts kicked in. "Run," it said. "Run." But I couldn't. My legs wouldn't move. I didn't know me not making this crucial decision would cost me everything.

Ewan Bennett (13)
St Boniface's Catholic College, Plymouth

Olympus Has Been Abandoned

The world was in turmoil. The earth shook with vigour. The titans, beasts sealed beneath earth by the gods, their prison of Tartarus was now empty. Atlas let go of the sky, Chronos rose again and Olympus was empty.

Those who could save them decided not to. Hades rose from the earth to reap the lives with Chronos' scythe, like Thanatos, taking lives as they began to take back what was once theirs. Taken. Taken by the mortal race. Taken by the gods before.

The world was in turmoil. The mortals had been extinguished. Olympus had now been abandoned.

Jacob Brewer (13)
St Boniface's Catholic College, Plymouth

The Beginning Of The End

It's been three weeks since it happened. The plague has consumed the whole of New York and I'm the last one standing. Everyone I know and love has become a mindless zombie.

I've figured out a pattern. They only come out in the dark and fear the sun. Daytime is the only time I can search for supplies and survivors. I've tried escaping but the government has walled it off.

Every night I barricade my doors and windows to keep myself safe from becoming one of them. I somehow have to survive until someone comes to help. Please save me.

Jack Greenhouse (13)
St Boniface's Catholic College, Plymouth

Gateway To Hell

Life couldn't get better. Everything I possibly ever wanted was in the grasp of my hands. I was well known in school and life was wonderful. I had great parents.
Until... the sirens went off. Ever since that catastrophe, my life turned upside down. All laws had been cut off since then. Gunshots, screams, bodies thudding against the floor. I did not think it was that much of a problem until my beloved parents were touched by the hands of death. I had revenge but the good feeling did not last long at all. That is when I heard the gunshot.

Kaif Ahmed (13)
St Boniface's Catholic College, Plymouth

Rabies 1929

I edged towards the tanks, soldiers only metres away.
Nearer and nearer, when they struck.

Waking up, vision blurred, I cleared my eyes. In front of me rats, the size of cats, crawled upon my body, biting me. Lice rippled through my hair. The sight of death overwhelmed me.

Rapidly, I went to speak to a soldier protecting the camp and showed the nastiness of my wounds. Not because he cared, he didn't care. However, I had been given an unknown disease, making the unknown plague that would be named rabies. Afterwards, I would die immediately.

Jack Bailey (12)
St Boniface's Catholic College, Plymouth

Untitled

On the Hiryū, April 6th 1944, taking off when I looked at the gauge. 70kmh, 80kmh, 100kmh. Seconds later, I was off patrolling the skies, bombs on my lap as I scoured the Pacific Ocean for the USS Yorktown. Deep breaths and pacing heartbeats overwhelmed me as I took my last breaths.

All of a sudden tracers fired past me. I looked into the distance as an SBD-3 Dauntless pulled up on my tail. My tail gone, soaring down. Luckily towards the Yorktown. Impact in three, two, one.

I pulled the pins off of the grenades. "Kamikaze!"

Finn Hawking (13)
St Boniface's Catholic College, Plymouth

Bartholemew

Bartholemew: kind, nice, amazing man. He had a beautiful black and white cat. The cat was young so Bartholemew walked his cat in his back garden.

Later that day, Bartholemew went to go get groceries for his dinner. He forgot the cat food so he went back. Strolling through the aisles, he found it. He paid and went home. While opening the door the cat, Ellie, ran out of the door and down the street. Bartholemew was very sad and didn't know what to do. He put up posters.

Defeated, he sat down. The doorbell rang. There she was.

Harvey McGrath (13)
St Boniface's Catholic College, Plymouth

The Siren

I was sitting in the classroom, and I heard a noise I had never heard before. The wailing siren pierced the atmosphere. It was time. The bomb had been dropped. I could see it hurtling towards the school from space. They were using the school grounds as a testing site for the new bomb. I heard the explosion and felt the heat; everything went dark.

I woke up. I survived. Everyone around me was dead, but I had a miracle and survived. The walls had disintegrated around me. I looked into the horizon and saw nothing anywhere. I was alone.

Jack Morton (14)
St Boniface's Catholic College, Plymouth

The Battle Of Humans And Monsters

I had sprinted out of my house with nothing to protect me from the bombs. The aliens and zombies flew around Earth, messing with our armies. I missed all my shots with my gun. Now I had to find shelter for my five-year-old brother. When I reloaded my gun it was just the UK left. The monsters got closer to land.

Ten minutes later, they took their first footsteps on concrete. Green slimy blood fell on my face. I was fighting for the world.

Now everyone was taken. Even my younger brother. Now, like Earth, I was screwed.

Seth Hawker (12)

St Boniface's Catholic College, Plymouth

The Recruitment

Today I woke up from a banging knock on my wooden door. So I sprinted downstairs thinking it was an emergency. I opened the door and there was this man in a military outfit. He said to me, "You have been recruited into the military to help us fight against Russia."
He pulled me out of the door and made me take off my clothes and shouted at me to put the military clothes on that he had brought. The man said, "What is your name, if I may ask?"
I answered, "Dunsin."
So it was time.

Jesudunsin Shoyemi (12)
St Boniface's Catholic College, Plymouth

Zombie Apocalypse

It all started when I went to test a patient with an antidote but this happened. "Raaarrr!" The patient screamed in a horrible voice, blood all over the patient's body and it broke free.

I ran away to my house. Then on the TV on the news, I saw zombies! I was scared. I didn't mean for this to happen. The breaking news was that the prime minister told everyone to evacuate the city but I was scared to go out.

Time went by and I went to kill zombies but I got bitten and I turned into a zombie.

Adeniran Praise Oluwadarasimi (11)

St Boniface's Catholic College, Plymouth

Surrounded

As I peered through the crack of the doorway all I could see was darkness fading over the walls of the buildings. But as the clock struck three, the mood changed from happy to dull. The screens on the walls turned on, gathering everyone's attention; the screens started playing and everyone stood there lifeless. The people started walking towards the screens like they were being controlled or brainwashed.

Suddenly, it was like the screens grew arms and latched around my body, pulling me in closer and closer.

Riley Coombe (13)
St Boniface's Catholic College, Plymouth

The Rapture

As I approached the extraterrestrial pod it slowly creaked open and I saw many red eyes and a writhing mass of robotic tentacles. As I stepped away, multiple tentacles shot out, stabbing and hooking the civilians around me. As blood and gore flew around me, other pods opened.
As I aimed my rifle at the mass it was slapped out of my hands by one of the robotic tentacles. Suddenly then I felt a sharp pain in my chest. I looked down and I saw a tentacle puncturing my stomach. I coughed up blood. I was dying.

Lucas Kaminski (13)
St Boniface's Catholic College, Plymouth

A Day Like Any Other?

It was 1939, a normal day at school. Or was it? All the teachers ran in and told us to duck under our desks. I was clueless. But then I found out what had happened. All the air raid sirens went off. My ears were ringing. *Bang!* I blacked out...

As I woke up I found myself on a bed. I didn't know where I was. It wasn't a hospital, I thought to myself. My eyes shut again.

They opened faintly. An old lady was standing in my face. She told me some really sad news. My parents had died!

Fletcher Newman (12)
St Boniface's Catholic College, Plymouth

The Murder Lights

It was a quiet Monday evening. I had no idea but the lights had shut off. After nineteen hours, the lights had not come on. I was terrified. Murders had been going on for hours. Then with a blink of an eye, the lights came on. It almost blinded me. All of the lights in my house flickered then just stayed on. My lamp next to my bed exploded from the heat. Then I heard more screams.

I ran back and looked outside of my window. Blood splattered over my new car and once again my front door opened...

Reagan Andrew (13)
St Boniface's Catholic College, Plymouth

The War Of Doom

The smoke cleared. Me and my pal were in the war. While we were shooting the enemy, my pal got shot. I was worried. I didn't know what to do.

I got the medicine from my bag. I took my shirt off and tied it around his arm. But the medicine didn't work. I saw my pal die in front of me.

Now it was only me in the war fighting for England. I started to hallucinate. I thought I was going crazy. I started to shoot the enemy and started to kill them all and became King David Peter.

David Makar (11)
St Boniface's Catholic College, Plymouth

Untitled

An asteroid hit the Earth and wiped out most of the human race. I was one of the survivors of the horrific incident. I was left with my son and my daughter but my wife died. I had to feed my children which was very hard, as well as looking after them. I had to kill animals to survive this disaster. All the shops had run out of food, water and other survival stuff.

Ten days later my daughter died from lack of food, water and viruses. Me and my son both buried her and put stones there.

Jack Harris (12)
St Boniface's Catholic College, Plymouth

WWIII Disaster

The smoke cleared. I could see something in the distance as I was heading to another warplane. I soon realised it was an English plane. I saw one of my fellow soldiers scared and about to pass out. There was not enough distance to turn so I had no choice but to jump out and leave him to die.
I grabbed my parachute and dived into the battlefield. Looking up at the flames, it exploded to pieces. I glided down feeling regret because I left a brave man behind. I landed safely.

Rocco Stronach (13)
St Boniface's Catholic College, Plymouth

The Year The UK Had Fallen

As sirens went off around I turned on the news and on the screen it said 'World War III' had broken out. I rushed to look out my window and then all I saw was bombs raining down. I rushed to my bunker. As I closed my bunker my house got hit. This meant I was in the middle of a catastrophe.

The next thing I heard was someone opening my door when I got dragged out into the army. After months of war, I was running as I was the last one. My country had lost...

Max Ball (12)
St Boniface's Catholic College, Plymouth

They All Die At The End

"I didn't mean for this to happen. I swear."

"Oh yeah, then why should I believe you? Look around, we can't even stop these deadly wolves."

"Guys," said Professor Sheniss.

"What?" said Doctor Aderson.

"I think I have an idea."

"Okay, then spit it out?"

"What if you bring them here and I start making something that makes them disappear?"

"Okay, fine, but it will be your fault if this doesn't work. Oh, and Doctor Smith, never do this again. Got it?"

And as we tried to get the deadly wolves to the headmaster he had something else in mind. Kill!

Faheem Kamara (11)
The Gatwick School, Crawley

Who's That?

"Welcome to the murder," as the man moved away.
"What happened?" I said with a look at the man. As I walked to Miss Rose's body I saw a person in the dark.
"Who's that?" Amma said, walking to the dark.
"Wait for me," Toby said, running to Amma.
"OMG, can you stop," said Jack, walking away.
"When was this?" I said looking at the man. The man said nothing and walked to the door.
"Where are you going?" Gus said, with a look.
"Yeah, where are you going, and I still need the time?" But the man only opened the door.

Ewan Watson (12)
The Gatwick School, Crawley

Thick Smoke

The thick smoke was choking! The room filled with grey clouds, filling up my lungs. I left the wooden spoon on the stove... The wooden spoon quickly caught alight and turned to an orange flame.

"What have I done? It's all my fault!" I was crawling along the floor, trying not to fill my body with smoke, barely breathing.

Then Mum walked through the door, smoke escaping from the kitchen.

"What happened?" she screamed, coughing through the smoke. Mum grabbed my arm and pulled me out of the house. We were fine, but the kitchen definitely wasn't.

Angel Aiken (12)

The Gatwick School, Crawley

Is This The End?

Was I the last one standing? People crouched down, coughing up blood as blotches bloomed on their skin. The smell of sickness filled the air as people in hazmat suits carried away casualties into blaring ambulances. I slung the mask around my ear as I watched children scream, groping for their parents. Full-grown adults clutched their stomachs, bending over in agony. I smiled in the chaos. People collapsed onto the dirt-covered pavement as panic rushed through the air. This was going perfectly. Everything was falling into place. I held up the only vaccination left. Who would get it?

Aisha Khan (13)
The Gatwick School, Crawley

A Big Fail

It was a normal day, I was getting ready for school when my friend texted, 'Have you revised for the test?'
I replied saying, 'What test?'
She answered, 'The maths test.'
'Oh god, I didn't prepare for any test and you're telling me it is today?'
She responded, 'They gave us two weeks to revise.'
I turned off my phone and panicked, grabbing a towel, soaking it in hot water and applying it to my forehead so I had a temperature and I tried my best to fake being sick!
Not knowing if I failed this test, I am dead!

Aimel Arif (12)
The Gatwick School, Crawley

Humanity's End

The Fourth War. The largest we've had since 1916. It was like every country turned on each other. An old organisation called NATO completely broke apart and everyone's family along with it.

I was around nineteen at the time. The TV warned us first, then our phones, then almost everything with a screen. They told us that politicians, soldiers and world leaders, they were all going insane.

We managed to drive to the middle of nowhere, me and my family. Then, we heard the whistling of the bombs around us. Screams echoed. Buildings fell. And one bomb fell on us.

Sydney Kazimierczak-Morfoot (13)
The Gatwick School, Crawley

Oopsie!

It was dark, the power just went out, funny. It was cold, too, but it was warm just a second ago; *how could it cool down so quickly?*

"Oopsie!" laughed an electronic voice that broke me out of my thoughts. It was female and taunting. "Sorry for the inconvenience." The power went back on. I decided it was just me and went on with my life.

It was fine for the next few days, but on the third day, the voice sounded again clearer and sassier, "My house now, pay rent or go!"

"How do I pay rent?" I asked.

Sumanohara Sai Sri Mallipudi (12)
The Gatwick School, Crawley

Alien Invaders

I didn't mean for this to happen. The aliens were on Earth. Was I the only one left? I couldn't see anybody else. I went to the button I pressed and realised it said 'Do Not Press!'. "Oh no," I said. I needed to find another button to press to get rid of these beasts.

I ran around this strange house trying so hard to find a button. At this point, there were aliens chasing me.

After all that running around, I finally found the button that would get these aliens away and bring the people back. "Hooray!"

Sophie Hemmant (11)
The Gatwick School, Crawley

Murphy

Everything about the day felt normal until they were spotted. God-like beings in the sky. Murphy was the first to sense them. He started randomly barking at the sky, or start growling trying to protect us. Everyone mockingly said, "What a silly rotweiler." Little did they know, the apocalypse was on its way...

Later that day, we saw them. They were like a mist of some sort. They had angelic wings and wore masks. We looked out the window only to see a wasteland of fire and rubble. We soon realised the only reason we were alive was... Murphy.

Jacob Byrne (12)
The Gatwick School, Crawley

The Day Of The Catastrophe

Today everything changed... Nobody knew this was going to happen. It was the day the storm came and destroyed everything.

It was early morning and everyone in the town was sleeping until *crash!* I jumped out of bed and looked out of my window. The oldest tree in the town had fallen onto the church. The wind gushed and the rain poured. No one expected this. The power was out. There were sirens. I was terrified. I wanted to escape, but I had no luck. I couldn't call anyone. I didn't know what to do. I hoped this had stopped, but no...

Amy Hussey (11)
The Gatwick School, Crawley

The Last Person Ever

Was I the only one left? I sprinted to Mum's room. "No! She's gone!" I ran to our neighbour, but she was gone too. I was scared, no one was there.

I walked into the city. Not a single person was around. I sat down on a bench. I slowly fell asleep, my head touching the cold wood.

I woke up. Looking around me, I saw nothing but the empty streets and shops. I quickly walked home, unlocked the door and turned on the television.

"No channels, try again!" I read out. Wait, was I the last person on Earth...?

Eliza Zorgji (12)
The Gatwick School, Crawley

The Holiday

My dad won four tickets to go to Mexico, one for me, my brother and Mum. We got stuck in a huge traffic jam on the way to the airport, and our hopes slowly drifted away, but then my mum called the airport and the lady on the phone said it would be okay if we were five minutes late.
We finally arrived at Gatwick Airport.
"I'm so excited!" I exclaimed. We went onto the plane.
Looking out the window, the plane finally took off and I got this feeling in my ears. Then I realised we had forgotten our suitcases.

Josh Parekh (12)
The Gatwick School, Crawley

The Plague

The lights went out. I thought I was safe now. It had been two weeks since the plague had spread across London, and there were few survivors.

While I sat in pitch black, the black death from 1665 crossed my mind. Why London of all places? Can't viruses go somewhere else? As I was in deep thought, a heavy weight landed on my shoulders. I turned and saw a lifeless face staring at me. A victim.

As I ran, a wave of tiredness crashed down on me. I tripped, landing next to a bin. I lay, realising I had the plague...

Isabella Stagg (11)
The Gatwick School, Crawley

Dystopia Girl!

Before I was born, there were stories about a girl. A girl just like me. Identical in every way. Same face, same eyes, same everything. This girl had the power to destroy the entire world. She could create dystopia.
I live here in dystopia. I have since I was seven. A girl whose anger could explode at any moment. A girl who was a ticking time bomb. I am the girl and the girl is me. I'm the girl who could burn the world. I was born as the girl with the power to destroy the world.

Skyla Allerton-Hilton (12)
The Gatwick School, Crawley

Lost Item

Yesterday, my dogs and I went to the woods; we needed some fresh air. I let one of my dogs off the lead, and he got lost. His name was Gadget; he had brown eyes and brown, soft ears. I called his name for hours, but he wouldn't come out, so my other dogs and I camped outside in a tent in the woods in case he came out, and he did. I was so happy and relieved he was okay. I gave him a big hug. So that was the story about a lost item.

Niamh Collins (12)
The Gatwick School, Crawley

Cardiac Arrests

Wednesday. Today there have been twelve thousand cardiacs already. What the heck happened? Me and Seasha have no clue.

At 02:00am an old man had a cardiac arrest. Seems pretty normal. Then it wasn't. Everyone else at the hospital started suffocating.

At 04:00am it had spread to London. The strangest thing is they're all fine. People woke up as fresh as a daisy. Albeit with a slight headache and weird loss of words about Tuesday. Why Tuesday?

Hang on, Seasha's calling me. Apparently, we've got to go to the vault. Which one? I have no clue. God, I hope it will be sorted out. Call ended.

Jaxson Shakir (13)
The Moulton School & Science College, Moulton

Steve's World

Was he the only one left?

A nuke had just been dropped on Northern America. A deadly virus was wiping people's brains, zombies! Plague 91 - a virus where radiation eats at your brain and zombifies people in close contact - had spread across America. Zombies tearing through flesh.

The only guy left in America had the IQ of a goldfish, Stubborn Steve. Would this guy be the guy to save the entire human population? Well, he isn't actually a human. Part of his skin had the virus but didn't progress. So, would he save us?

Jake Smith (14)
The Phoenix Collegiate, West Bromwich

The Concealing Plague

Am I the only one left? Everyone is missing; no one is in sight. Walking along the isolated, gloomy streets of London, I make sure my yellow hazard suit and gas mask are tightly wrapped around my body. Making sure not to let the deadly poison-filled air attack my body by seeping its way through the creases. I cautiously make my way to what was once a busy town, now an abandoned, concealed place.

Kelsey Bushell (14)
The Phoenix Collegiate, West Bromwich

Plague

"Breaking News! The prime minister has ordered a mandatory lockdown for everyone living in London. The grass plague is spreading rapidly throughout the city, killing everyone who catches it. The plague kills people by stopping the blood from going around the body."
Dave watched the announcement, horrified. Dave said to himself, "Is this the end?"

Charlie Walden (13)
The Phoenix Collegiate, West Bromwich

Is It True?

One text changes everything. Oscar and I were a perfect couple. Everyone at school loved us. But last night, I got a text from an unknown number saying, 'Oscar cheated on you' and they proceeded to send photos of him kissing other girls.
Should I confront him? What if this is fake? These thoughts flooded my head. What should I do?

Melissa Diggins (14)
The Phoenix Collegiate, West Bromwich

Shadows Of Strife

In the throes of geographical strife, Russia's expansionist desires clashed fiercely with the UK's resolute stance. The trigger contested territories in Eastern Europe.
Diplomatic channels faltered, igniting a relentless conflict. Across battlefields, the thunderous clamour of tanks mingled with the cries of soldiers.
From the icy expanses of Ukraine to London's urban landscape, each side fought fervently for supremacy. Amidst the chaos, alliances shifted like sand in a desert storm. Covert operations, spying and treachery became common. Yet amidst the devastation, stories of heroism surfaced as brave souls defended their homelands with unyielding valour.
Ultimately, the war made scars on Britain.

Jorge William Martin (11)
Tunbridge Wells Grammar School for Boys, Tunbridge Wells

Sixty Seconds To Run

"Shoot!" Bob blurted out. "That's the wrong substance! Do you know what that was?"

"That's combodium!" I retorted. "That'll make this whole birthday combust in sixty seconds! We have to evacuate everyone!"

Hastily, we bolted to the nearest alarm and pulled it. Fifty seconds left.

Everyone nearby was panicking. "No time to mess about!" I yelled. "Get out of here!" Forty seconds left.

A flock of scientists dashed through the narrow halls. Thirty metres from the exit: twenty-five seconds left.

"Help!" Someone had tripped over. Bob and I heaved him up, taking ten seconds.

Exit!

Five... four... three... two... one...

Jenson Tatton
Tunbridge Wells Grammar School for Boys, Tunbridge Wells

The Last Day On The Earth

Five minutes... five minutes until the fiery, smouldering asteroid hit, destroying everything in London.
"I can see it!" exclaimed my mother. "Speed up!" she commanded my father.
"Four minutes!" I proclaimed.
As I looked around the once peaceful park I remember playing in as a child, it became a compacted battleground of people, fighting to keep the city.
"Three minutes, we won't make it."
"Two minutes."
Ahead of us, the road was closed by the police! We took a left... closed, right... closed! We got out and sprinted away from the danger.
"One minute. Thirty seconds."
I was too late!

Edward Oliver (13)
Tunbridge Wells Grammar School for Boys, Tunbridge Wells

Untitled

Sirens blared. The wind stormed through the neighbourhood, catapulting branches in every direction. Trees shook wildly, barely hanging onto their roots. Rain plummeted to the ground as though it were hail.
The tornadoes had finally reached Alex's home as he ran as fast as he could back to his parents' arms. His parents waited for him in the doorway, uneasily. By the time Alex got inside, the tornado raged outside, moments away. "Bye Mom, bye Dad, thank you for everything." Silence.
"The tornado has disappeared." Cheers flooded the street as crowds of people celebrated. "Oh, looks like there's no Wi-Fi! Nooo!"

James Jaswal (12)
Tunbridge Wells Grammar School for Boys, Tunbridge Wells

Scorched

Spotted outside the lockers, bags in hand, Chad Chuckwell. The locker slammed. The victim screamed. The lights went out. The crowd emerged out of the doors, and orange, scorching, spiky gas erupted down the hallways as it cackled in rage.

Ambulance sirens wailed as big Chuckwell raced out onto the pavement. Screaming, crying and shouting were coming from the building. Smoke burst from the room as civilians screeched, jaywalking over the road. The school fell apart, cars were in flames and unconscious people were tightly locked inside crushed taxis.

Suddenly a great oil can burst out onto someone quickly. A shriek came out. Chad Chuckwell, gone.

Raff Curtis (13)

Tunbridge Wells Grammar School for Boys, Tunbridge Wells

Mafia Murder!

Bang!
The Brutus organisation had shot two rocketing bullets,
dealing a decisive blow to the Stanely Mafia heads!
"No!" wailed Arthur Stanely in the most gut-wrenching
manner.
Suddenly two of the organisation's bodyguards immediately
dug their bloody fingers into Arthur's shoulders, dragging
him to an unknown place. He was gone.
Sobbing and sobbing against the unbreakable tomb walls,
Arthur bellowed for sympathy, but the spiteful silhouettes
swallowed his wails. Arthur's hopes had been crushed. He
was stuck there forever. He was doomed. Was this meant to
be? Was this the end for young Arthur?

Ethan Tran (11)
Tunbridge Wells Grammar School for Boys, Tunbridge Wells

Into The Unknown

Johnny felt unrealism flying through the mist. As he saw many dimensions upon him, he fell into one.
In the music dimension, dissonance ripped through melodies, clattering harmonies. He fell into another.
Fortnite's battles warped into a surreal nightmare as guns shot beside him. Then, paint splashed chaotic patterns across the canvas realm.
Each dimension by the next, unravelling the consequences he had done. Shattering his own dimension; seeing the fabric of the Earth disappear among his own eyes.
Shameless, he knew that he would be stuck continuously teleporting through different dimensions unless... Wait, there was an exit!

David Efimov (13)
Tunbridge Wells Grammar School for Boys, Tunbridge Wells

Magic's End

The aura dispersed. The glittering sunlight vanished. Neko sensed the magic drain, creeping through the Witching Woods. As trees clawed at the wizard cat, the crystal of magic shattered. Neko was told by a merchant.

Wading through Spell Marsh, Neko fought a magical battle with a dragon. Neko rested in a mushroom village, Cap Heights, inhabited by frogs. Neko reached a cave seeping glowing blue light. Tiptoeing in, Neko noticed a blue gem in pieces.

"I see you've arrived," a dog witch, named Inu, cackled. Inu broke the crystal.

Neko battled her, the crystal supplying magic. Neko succeeded and fixed it.

Thomas Garcia (13)
Tunbridge Wells Grammar School for Boys, Tunbridge Wells

The Never Again Scotland

The government wanted no one alive! In Scotland, a frizzy morning, gloom took over nature, smothering trees. I fancied a stroll. Gummy mud rose on my feet.
5am. Sirens had come, faint. Its sounds came closer.
Later, the sight of riots. I felt apprehensive. Anxious, I hid in a nearby crumbling war bunker. Rats sprawled around, thinking they were disease Deliveroo drivers.
Thirty minutes passed, still sirens. A scream caught my attention, coming from the village. *Boom!* Great ashes drove into the air. Aircrafts swarmed, wiping out cities. The world shook, for hell had happened. It was over. I knew I was next.

Rory White
Tunbridge Wells Grammar School for Boys, Tunbridge Wells

Untitled

Yesterday, everything changed. I looked out the window and I saw it. Daleks, spiders and aliens, they destroyed the planet. Everything except our house. They were circling us, repeating, "Protect the chosen one."
Then suddenly, they took me.
I was abducted. I saw my parents, they were waiting for me. Then they said, "Today is the day." They said, "You become King."
I was confused but then I realised I was royalty. There was unknown technology. I became a universal explorer. There was a map saying, 'Let the adventure begin.'
I was off. Then I woke up and then... school.

Dexter Howie (12)
Tunbridge Wells Grammar School for Boys, Tunbridge Wells

A Father And A Son

As the dust cleared, revealing buildings brought to their knees, a ringing pierced through the silence and clogged my ears. As I trudged upon the bloodstained rubble, it hit me. I remembered the ground shaking, skyscrapers collapsing, leaving a cloud of dust to hide the bodies. I scanned the area frantically and caught a glimpse of a sign reading, 'Covid-19 Facility. Keep Out.'

Trembling, I limped towards the white tent and coughs infested my ears, and lying on the floor were white suits wearing strange masks. They weren't empty.

My stomach dropped when I saw him motionless. My only son, motionless.

Oscar Brooks-Wilkins (13)
Tunbridge Wells Grammar School for Boys, Tunbridge Wells

Journey To Paradise

As the sun darkened, the plane's engines stuttered, and 140 passengers didn't know what was coming for them. Peacefully I drifted off, expecting to be woken in paradise. Suddenly I woke up to a *bang!* The seatbelt sign flickered, trying its hardest to turn on. In a flash, the captain came through the PA. In a glitchy tone, he exclaimed, "Passengers, lightning has struck our engines, and on top of that, our left wing is detached! Put your oxygen mask on immediately." However, the oxygen masks didn't appear. As I held my breath, shuddering, I rushed into the cockpit. There was no pilot...

Orlando Clement (13)
Tunbridge Wells Grammar School for Boys, Tunbridge Wells

Nothing Is Real

Everyone wants me dead. I met with Putin and we spoke. I must've said something that enraged him and he was threatening nuclear war. That is why everyone hates me. I have nobody.

Shortly before that happened someone in shaggy clothing sold me pills and now I'm here. These white cushioned walls are splendid but this guard says I'm in a mental hospital, whatever that means.

Then Jack said, "Stop taking these pills, you're killing yourself."

What?

"You're hallucinating, this isn't real. You killed me and you never met Putin."

But who's the guard then?

Aadam Chatha (13)
Tunbridge Wells Grammar School for Boys, Tunbridge Wells

The Gorillas Who Escaped The Zoo

Bang! Crash! Thud! The big, black gorillas escaped the zoo, rampaging through the streets, everyone hiding inside as the big, black, abominable monsters roamed the streets. Smashing the windows, picking up people and cars and throwing them around and robbing stores for their food when they get hungry. Breaking into jewellery stores so gorillas can get a necklace.

On the news, a gorilla climbed up a massive building. Everyone was told to evacuate until he jumped off onto a fighter jet which crashed into a nearby building.

The gorillas were all captured and sent back to the zoo after all that trouble.

Lewis Hook (13)
Tunbridge Wells Grammar School for Boys, Tunbridge Wells

The Broken Soldier

Bullets flew past me, skimming my jaw. I howled in agony. A grenade was thrown. *Bang!*
Fire sailed up into the air, dancing around like ballerinas. Mayhem was happening, people running, debris flying everywhere.
"Ow!" Shards of glass slid into me like a knife through butter.
Blood trickled down my face, blurring my vision. An invisible force hit me, throwing me back onto the ground. For a brief second, I was blinded, my ears buzzing.
I got up slowly, my ankle was broken, twisted 180 degrees. A bone sticking out. I limped painfully to the nearest shelter, but the roof collapsed.

Oliver Clark (11)
Tunbridge Wells Grammar School for Boys, Tunbridge Wells

Coconut Storm

It was a pleasant morning. Igor strolled through the park, thinking about his nightmares. A thought he had always hated was coconuts falling from the sky.

The dry ground crunched as he walked along the path, but something felt peculiar. The air was humid, the sky felt as if it was going to collapse. Igor, expecting the worst, looked up and got the nightmare he always feared.

Brown balls blasted through the sky. They cracked on the pavement, creating rivers of cloudy water. Coconuts started hitting him and Igor fell into a trance.

Next thing he knew, he was falling.

James Burdis (13)
Tunbridge Wells Grammar School for Boys, Tunbridge Wells

Death By Big Mac

I drop my pink drink. "Oh!" The pavement drops and makes a clunk noise. It's probably just a loose stone.

Later, I'm watching the news. It says, "Meteorologists have discovered that huge Big Macs are moving towards us at an alarming rate, with a direct collision course! Unless they're stopped, they'll hit in fourteen hours and destroy all life!" Videos of Big Macs dodging missiles are shown on the screen.

At night, the Big Macs are here. They're the last things I see. "Uh, oh, spaghettios!"

It was all my fault. They were sent by the pink drink.

Joseph Tyler (12)
Tunbridge Wells Grammar School for Boys, Tunbridge Wells

How Humanity Destroyed Itself

I can't believe it happened. We survived, but it cost us. We were lucky, we were very lucky. Or were we?
The aftermath is horrible, dead bodies in piles, buildings utterly destroyed and survivors left distraught. The catastrophe happened a few days back. We weren't expecting it, and more importantly... we weren't prepared. It started when electronic devices started to behave strangely and then they began to have a mind of their own. Soon after, devices took over the world and used nuclear weapons to destroy what was left. That was how humanity was erased and was turned into extinction.

Alex Martin (13)
Tunbridge Wells Grammar School for Boys, Tunbridge Wells

Falling Into Fate

My mind whizzed... Blackness.

I gradually grew back my consciousness. Spine-chilling screams echoed around me. In front of my car, a ferocious fire roared at me. Hurriedly, I tried shoving open the door... but... I couldn't! Fear filled my soul. What was I to do? Suddenly, a cable from the bridge snapped! My car crept forwards on the crumbling platform. Beside me, panicking people rushed off, carrying their phones, clothes, some even with babies! With much force, I attempted to now kick open the door... It wouldn't budge...

Another cable snapped! Was this it? My car leaned over the edge...

William Underwood (13)
Tunbridge Wells Grammar School for Boys, Tunbridge Wells

Meteor In London

"Breaking News, astronomers have discovered an asteroid rushing towards Earth!"

It has been ages since that broadcast. The asteroid hit London only weeks ago, causing an everlasting famine and plague to hit England.

The disease has been named Meteoritis and has wiped out most of our population. Also, we have to eat what's left in supermarkets to survive.

Locked inside the store for safety, trembling, I reflected on my life.

Suddenly, I felt an enormous gust of wind on my neck. I glanced behind me and realised that the door was open.

I started to cough. It all went black...

Rupert Walton (11)

Tunbridge Wells Grammar School for Boys, Tunbridge Wells

Failed

"Our Prime Minster, Thorpe Johnson, has announced a government operation has failed. We will soon be gone."
I looked at my mother. She stared at the television, horror-struck and disturbed. The sky went red. We heard explosions in the distance along with screams of fear. Sirens wailed. The television had cut off. All lights were gone.
"What's happening?" I asked Mother.
"We don't have time! Pack your bags and go to the cellar."
I began to weep. The world was falling apart. I never thought this day would come. Then, they found us. *Knock. Knock.*

Max Frith (12)
Tunbridge Wells Grammar School for Boys, Tunbridge Wells

Mission, Get Me Out Of Here

War. Destruction. Chaos.

This was the last two months of my life. Terrorist troops patrolled the grief-stricken, destructed streets. Another squad passed as I scuttled across the street.

"Hey," they shouted, but I was already gone. This was my ticket out of here, and all I had to do was make it to the helicopter.

I saw it land and launched myself across the field onto the vehicle.

"Alright, Wolf?" I asked.

"Not bad, now let's go!" he replied.

We were off, flying into the skies, then a rumble. We plummeted to the ground and everything went dark.

Matthew Drane (13)

Tunbridge Wells Grammar School for Boys, Tunbridge Wells

Dingleberry Needs Saving

Despair. Dingleberry is lost. Empty streets, poor children pleading for a saviour, malnourished and all alone.
Many used to live here but it's now a ghost town, even the rich live in poverty, drinking at the bars, whisky and moonshine in hand. All is lost...
Except a furry friend has come to help, a short chestnut coat, wet black nose and the tenacity to help have shown the difference between him and others.
His cries had brought people from town to town and his unintimidating looks were the complete opposite of what you would expect.
The true saviour of Dingleberry is here to help.

Tom Binks (14)
Tunbridge Wells Grammar School for Boys, Tunbridge Wells

It's The Unknown

"Breaking news, the prime minister has announced that the most life-threatening disease has been found in the Arctic. Climate change has gotten so bad that a mutated bubonic plague has taken over."

His eyes shot open. James saw the news and knew what happened. After seventy years and billions wasted, Rishi had stepped down. Honks blared on the road, cars crashed and everyone needed to leave. Now!

James packed and went for the helicopter on the roof, heading for Hawaii. He had a bunker ready to go to.

With a crash, the helicopter landed on the rough sand. The door wouldn't open.

Oscar White (13)
Tunbridge Wells Grammar School for Boys, Tunbridge Wells

The New Era

6:00am.

We woke to singing sirens, so I knew only one thing could have happened. War! Immediately, I sprinted for the fridge. If I was going to survive I needed food, water and shelter, or else the radiation would sneak inside and burn me inside out.

Unfortunately, millions would experience it, maybe billions. Who knew? Suddenly, I went blind.

My eyes were boiling and screeching in pain. Nevertheless, I bolted down to the apartment lobby, calling for others to join me. Only five followed me, only five could comprehend the situation.

Only five would survive the apocalyptic new era...

Zachary Bonval (13)
Tunbridge Wells Grammar School for Boys, Tunbridge Wells

The Virus

It was 2099. Everyone was anticipating the new century. However, we didn't know it was the end of our lives on Earth.

With the social media industry booming, aliens were expanding their own technologies. Although this wasn't enough for those greedy creatures, they wanted to have more power.

The aliens were ambitious, as they went forward in destroying social media and us. They hacked our systems, planting a virus in the database. It spread like wildfire.

In only an hour, news leaked, telling everyone not to go on social media, aliens were now superior. Was it the end though...?

Finlay Heffernan (12)
Tunbridge Wells Grammar School for Boys, Tunbridge Wells

The Internet Plague

"Three, two, one, we're reporting live now. Evidence of a new virus is spreading. It's believed to have been caused by addictive social media platforms. Our advice is to turn off your internet."

The internet-caused plague was taking over: humans were foaming through their mouths and turning extremely pale after watching short videos, mainly on platforms like TikTok. Over half the population had fallen - only extreme tribes and isolated places remained... but for how long? The end was near! Humans left were depressed with no hope. The people were lost in their minds, but then...

Louis Dennis (12)
Tunbridge Wells Grammar School for Boys, Tunbridge Wells

Time

Sprint faster, I thought. I used all my energy and ran through the park and happy families playing football and sunbathing with no care in the world.

As I turned the corner, I saw the holy place I very much desired. This was the final stretch. I could almost smell it. As I ran through the door, I ordered it. "£4.99, that's gone up."

I patiently waited until I heard my number. *Will it taste as good? I hope so*, I thought.

"Order 133," the man called.

I stepped outside with my order. I opened the bag.

My chicken nuggets. Yum.

George Cunningham (14)
Tunbridge Wells Grammar School for Boys, Tunbridge Wells

Worst Day Ever

This was it. The final day of waiting. I was getting the brand new iPhone 27. Filled with excitement, I gleefully strolled down the energetic street. Within sight, the majestic Apple store awaited. Horror struck me. Engulfed in raging flames, my blood boiled - it was closed. Why would it be closed on a Saturday?

I calmed myself down. After, I remembered there was one down Brick Lane, only three miles away.

Ring, ring, my mum wouldn't pick up!

A taxi! I thought.

Finally, I had arrived, yet this time it was open. Reaching in for my wallet, my card was gone!

Luke Williams (13)
Tunbridge Wells Grammar School for Boys, Tunbridge Wells

The Rumble

I was walking home when it happened. I was kicking a jagged pebble along the ruined pavement, bored out of my mind, when the ground quivered.

It shook inexplicably, almost vibrating. Then more, and more! The whole road was shaking, swaying side to side. Speeding up as it trembled, cracks spread along the tarmac. The chasm widened, expanding like an infected cut.

The ground was shaking violently. As I struggled to keep my footing, terror spread across my face at what I saw. The buildings to my right were splitting, howling, crumbling into cracked ruins.

Our planet started to rumble.

Marco Mellinger (13)
Tunbridge Wells Grammar School for Boys, Tunbridge Wells

The Rig

Now they were pumping, Timothy considered his job done. However, as he turned to leave it shivered and creaked. Suddenly, the pipe burst and oil-covered creatures burst from the rupture, attacking them. The nearest person screamed and fell back in terror.

Timothy turned to run, but one of the ungodly horrors blocked his path. It was about thirty centimetres tall and slick with oil. It growled threateningly and received three firm whacks with a spanner.

Timothy sprinted for the lifeboats, praying one was still there. There was one left, packed with people. He just managed to leap aboard.

Sebastian White (14)
Tunbridge Wells Grammar School for Boys, Tunbridge Wells

The Cyber Attack

There was a London cyber attack. Nobody knew what was happening. Electricity was going on and off. People panicked. But a boy with lots of IT knowledge was contacted and he got to work immediately.

After two months, the boy had already found suspects but couldn't figure out who it was. He was given all the information needed. Only one person stood out. Reginald Eggburn. He broke out of three prisons by hacking the prison servers. He could easily do a cyber attack on London. When the boy told the government about Reginald all information (including his birth certificate) was deleted.

Orhan Imad Murad (11)
Tunbridge Wells Grammar School for Boys, Tunbridge Wells

The Monster

Ready... launching. A bomb the size of a mountain launches towards the desert. Loud screeching starts. A cloud of blood-red fog appears. The fog surrounds the desert and a rumble starts.

An island on the coast of Russia shakes. A cave is set ablaze. It was an eye... An intimidating crimson eye. It moves an inch and an avalanche of rocks fall. Boulders cascade in the sky. A large black figure rises out of the ground.

Suddenly, the island submerges. *Bang!* An explosion collides with the monster's impenetrable skin. It falls into the sea. One last bubble and reality collapses.

Tom Moriaty-Cole (12)

Tunbridge Wells Grammar School for Boys, Tunbridge Wells

Saved By A Miracle Power Plant

My heart raced when I witnessed the heat of the core reactor. Everyone had already evacuated, but I wouldn't let it explode. The temperature crawled towards 12,000°C. I opened the emergency controls without hesitation as the cooling pipes started to seep out the cooling fluid.

To activate emergency shutdown, I needed the keys so I ran to the storage room and opened the key cupboard. I then sprinted back amidst the fire and inserted the key, my eyes burning. I ran to the bunker as the huge door sealed and checked the estimated time to explosion.

3... 2... 1... Shutdown. Success!

Edward Nunn (12)
Tunbridge Wells Grammar School for Boys, Tunbridge Wells

Chaos!

"Breaking news, the election of Prime Minister is chaotic."
As soon as this reached my ears, a cold shiver ran through
my whole body. I was at the rear of the crowd when
suddenly, smoke slowly drifted into the clear sapphire sky.
Instantly a warm flame jumped from the ground into the
heavens. Rapidly, I reached into my pocket for my phone.
Petrified I read on the screen 'no battery!'. Abruptly, I
started sprinting as fast as my legs would go, my brain,
concentrating on one thing, how speedily I could reach the
police and safety.
I woke sweating, it was a dream.

Hadrien Mauduit (11)
Tunbridge Wells Grammar School for Boys, Tunbridge Wells

Monsters On The Streets

In a time when the sky burned red, giant creatures from another world enslaved our kind.

A brave boy explored the abandoned streets for supplies with his dog. Explosions and screams filled the air as he ventured deeper. The buildings were crumbled. The stench of fire burned his nose and the rocks were breaking into his shoes.

He found a store full of snacks and food. When he opened the door a dark aura filled his and the dog's heads. Something was there, looking at them in the shadows. Red eyes appeared around them as a light shot down.

"No, please. No, dammit..."

George Hale (12)
Tunbridge Wells Grammar School for Boys, Tunbridge Wells

My Last Breath

Breaking news, the prime minister had declared conflict with Russia. *Boom!* A noxious, toxic bomb struck Downing Street. I lived just a couple of minutes away. Fire and blackness spread throughout the streets.

Was I in a dream? After attempting to wake up, I realised... it was reality. The rapidly expanding smoke got closer. Connections with the prime minister were totally lost.

I dashed. Darkness grew around me. I was choking in the dense smoke. What was happening? An explosion? Had Russia struck already? I was not certain but one thing I was sure of... I could not breathe.

Taylor Jones (12)
Tunbridge Wells Grammar School for Boys, Tunbridge Wells

F1 Heartbreak

The entire world watching me, I have to show them. I step into my dream car, the majestic, lightning-fast Ferrari Veneno.

Three, two, one, go! I'm off, my engine roars and my heart pounds. No one is as fast as I am. I'm speeding down the track, third to second. My excitement taking over, I haven't noticed the brake lights in front. I press down on the brakes. Nothing happens. The distance between us is incredibly short.

Smoke rises, blinding me, impairing my breathing.

I wake. The doctor has arrived with news: "I'm sorry, we had to amputate your leg."

Noah White (12)
Tunbridge Wells Grammar School for Boys, Tunbridge Wells

How?

Suddenly, all the lights turned off. A shooting star (it seemed) was enclosing London. Everything was icy... Flowers were frozen. As I looked up, the shooting star had started circling Big Ben. A huge cloud grew, it surrounded the star, making it invisible.

When I checked my phone, it went straight to a screen where the prime minister explained, "London's in trouble. Stay indoors!"

Abruptly, I felt a shudder under the soles of my feet. Fated to find out what was going on, I ventured forward. Unexpectedly, I heard a bang. Somehow, Big Ben had fallen. "Oh no!"

Fred Kolbe (12)

Tunbridge Wells Grammar School for Boys, Tunbridge Wells

End Of The World

Breaking News, the prime minister has declared an asteroid is heading straight for New York City. Everyone must get in their bunkers and hide as the foreseeable future could be deadly. You should probably grab the supplies you need now before the world collapses into darkness. A pit of doom that you can't escape.

We are just getting information from the space station and NASA headquarters that the asteroid is travelling at 2x the speed of light through the atmosphere as we speak. This could end humanity, especially now we have 3 hours until destruction so run and hide for your life.

Leo Seadon (12)
Tunbridge Wells Grammar School for Boys, Tunbridge Wells

The Disease

Boom! The test tube exploded. An alarm sounded and scientists ran in all directions. The boy crouched behind a bin. Why didn't he stay home, like he was supposed to?
"Miles!" his father cried as he ran past. "Why aren't you at home?"
Another explosion sounded. A tsunami of sound hit him and he was sent flying. Flames engulfed him as purple goo seeped out of the cracks in the ceiling, dripping onto his burnt face.
"Oh no!" his father sobbed as he knelt beside his dying child.
Suddenly, Miles opened his eyes.
His purple eyes.

Samuel Chamberlain (12)
Tunbridge Wells Grammar School for Boys, Tunbridge Wells

Don't Lose Hope

The gunshots rang in my ears. Explosions shook the earth around me. My parents, brother and I huddled beneath the soil, just in a metal box. Perhaps waiting for our doom. Dive-bomber planes screamed as they came down, encasing horror in our souls. With the thick smoke above, it seemed like the day would not come.

The yells of agony from soldiers scarred us, piercing our hearts.

After what seemed like a lifetime, we left the shelter. Our eyes were met by an unrecognisable, ruined landscape. Yet through the clouds of smoke, the sun could be seen, shining, bringing fresh happiness.

Connor Fairless (12)

Tunbridge Wells Grammar School for Boys, Tunbridge Wells

9Lives

"Brand new, the revolutionary piece of technology, 9Lives!" the TV blurted.

My 9Lives chip had already arrived and my mum and I had nearly finished setting it up. Finally, it was complete. I couldn't wait. I stuffed the chip into my ear: I could feel the power inside already. Twenty-four hours was the wait time when it was usable.

As I went into my bed my mind started to go crazy. My legs carried me away. I started to run in the other direction. It was useless. I wasn't in control anymore. The 'revolutionary device' had hypnotised everyone. It was over.

Leo Heathcoat (12)
Tunbridge Wells Grammar School for Boys, Tunbridge Wells

Apocalyptic Chaos

"Emergency! Evacuation plan activated!" said the Mayor of London.

There was an apocalyptic chaos happening around the whole city. A blanket of black smoke covered every part of light in the day, wiping out any sight of the sun that was available.

Suddenly, there was noise and banging at our front door. My father looked through the spyhole and saw a horde of zombies! We barricaded the doors and ran to the basement armed with baseball bats and other supplies of food and water. We heard a smashing window and instantly knew that the zombies were coming, but we were ready!

Luca Woolger (12)
Tunbridge Wells Grammar School for Boys, Tunbridge Wells

The Fall Of The Living

Darkness fell upon Greece, but this time a black cloud of smoke choked the people. The rumbling under everyone's feet made them stutter and stumble. An evil laugh, followed by three howls, was heard in the distance.

Shortly after, everything returned to its original state. Well, that's what they thought. The whole of Mykonos had drastically changed. What once was a luscious island was now a toxic barren wasteland. All trees were defenseless and the rivers had turned to a dark green colour. Every living soul that was in Mykonos had turned into skulls. The underworld was here.

Harry Mauldon (12)
Tunbridge Wells Grammar School for Boys, Tunbridge Wells

The Darkness Above

"Go, go!" cheered Philip, the single father of the once orphaned child. As the son was about to score the winning ball, a darkness flooded the skies and field.

Philip slowly leaned up and gazed at the sky, covering his eyes with his roughened hands. He saw a flaming ball flying down. He almost instantaneously sprinted for his son.

It was too late! Hours after, he awakened and reached out of the rubble and frantically searched for his beloved son, even though he was seriously injured.

He searched and searched, but found no luck.

Philip fell to his wounded knees.

Benjamin Wackett (13)

Tunbridge Wells Grammar School for Boys, Tunbridge Wells

Roman Destroyer Of Big Macs' Great Rescue

The date was September 11th 2001; the world-renowned time traveller Roman, destroyer of Big Macs, was on the scene ready to stop the horrible event that changed many people's lives forever. He dressed in the clothes they wore in the early 2000s and booked a very cheap ticket for their time; he immediately spotted all four terrorists and cautiously placed sensor trackers on all of them.
When the time was right, Roman pounced like a tiger and refused the terrorists' orders, easily beating them to the ground. After all the terrorists were defeated, he landed the plane safely.

Leo Thomas (13)
Tunbridge Wells Grammar School for Boys, Tunbridge Wells

Animatronics Arise

The lights shut off. I had run out of power despite my best efforts. I had failed to survive the onslaught. The pirate fox, the blue rabbit, the yellow chicken and the brown bear, all gone rogue. After terrorising the locals, haunting the town's essence, it was my turn.

However, as they drew closer, and my end drew nearer, I noticed something. The springlock suit. Knowing I had no option, I put it on, knowing I'd live on. Alas, the combination of my quivering, combined with the leaky building, was too much. Just as the animatronics arrived, the springlocks snapped shut...

Jacob Ashlee (13)
Tunbridge Wells Grammar School for Boys, Tunbridge Wells

The Day The Sun Fell

The sky was a pale grey. The air scratched my throat with each breath. Something rose, warming my face. It crept closer, over buildings. Everything around me was set ablaze. I felt fragile, like nobody was around to save me.

The smoke advanced down my throat. Everything around me was dissolved by the everlasting inferno until I stood in a sweltering circle of fire. My rubber shoes liquified into the concrete pavement, restricting my movement.

The wave of fire charged towards me, trying to quench its insatiable hunger. My lips were the first to dry. Then my eyes. And then...

Jamie Bothwell (13)
Tunbridge Wells Grammar School for Boys, Tunbridge Wells

Untitled

I woke up to hear the song of war striking its first note. Raging flames enveloped the capital as the fire of anti-aircraft guns boomed in the distance.

"It didn't have to happen. I refused to do it now everybody pays the price."

Tears welled up in my eyes as I watched this scene of merciless havoc. The hellish machines of war had set to work to wreck, ruin and desolation. A missile elegantly whistled past, only to raid a sprawling hospital.

"I can't take it any longer."

Death was the only escape. I looked out the window... and jumped.

Aleksander Hajdukovic (12)
Tunbridge Wells Grammar School for Boys, Tunbridge Wells

The End Is Near

Bang! A huge green mushroom cloud burst up from the site of the nuclear plant.

I rushed over to the gate to see what happened but from the iron bars, I saw something strange... The people inside were alive!

Suddenly, across the sky, four huge beams of light soared up and turned the sky blood red. The workers inside started shuffling over. "Hi guys, everything alright?" I called out. Stepping into the light, their deformed faces with pulsing pus bubbles gleamed in the sun, organs drooping out of their chests.

At that moment, I knew it was the end...

Caleb Jackson (11)

Tunbridge Wells Grammar School for Boys, Tunbridge Wells

WWIII Breakout

The prime minister had reported that countries were fighting across the world. "Is this the start of WWIII?"
The swinging of a sword and the booming of a gun went on forever. Fighting all day and all night. Now bombs and tanks covered the whole battlefield. Then I was recruited for war. I had guns, landmines and outfits. I was ready. Fighting all day, attacking all day, I even had to defend.
It happened faster than ever. There my body was, dead on the field.
"We are here to respect the life of this fallen soldier. Goodbye, my friend. Miss you."

Louie Groves (11)
Tunbridge Wells Grammar School for Boys, Tunbridge Wells

Aliens Vs Me

Disaster struck, and China was at war with aliens. Missiles were launched everywhere and one hundred million people died. The aliens were far more advanced so they were winning the war, but then China had a glimpse of hope as they saw soldiers and fighter jets from America, Russia, The UK, France, South Korea, Japan, Italy and India fight off the aliens.

Would that be enough to win the war? No, they needed the most powerful being in this universe. Me! With a flick of my fingers, I wiped all the aliens away from Earth, saving the world and permanently destroying all aliens.

Luca Bonval (11)
Tunbridge Wells Grammar School for Boys, Tunbridge Wells

A War-torn City

Berlin, 2048.

I stooped down behind the rubble, which was once a warm home. My arm was bleeding and I could see blood on the street.

Suddenly, a bullet like the one that previously cut my arm came hurtling just over my head.

I yelled, "Ahh!" as I dived amongst the rubble.

The sky was a blood red, as the last streams of daylight disappeared behind the very few remaining buildings left.

As darkness clutched the city, all I could hear was gunshots cutting through the night.

I thought for a second, *what has happened to this world*?

Samuel Philpott (12)
Tunbridge Wells Grammar School for Boys, Tunbridge Wells

Chemical Plague

This morning, the prime minister announced that an untested chemical had been released in an accident, but he assured us that the situation was under control...
Ten minutes later, I got back up from bed after deciding that the news was too boring, to the horrific noise of car alarms. I saw that a deer had bumped my neighbour's car so I pulled out my camera for a photo.
Crash! I saw that a hunk of flesh had broken through a wall and consumed the deer.
Bang! I shot off a chunk of meat from the beast and watched it become its own Colossus...

Alfie Elliott (12)
Tunbridge Wells Grammar School for Boys, Tunbridge Wells

The Day Everything Changed

Running. Can't stop, won't stop, now with Mum gone. To think, today was going to be great. We were in the park, then the unthinkable happened.

Scary black holes started coming out of the ground. They started to suck everything under. I saw our whole neighbourhood running away.

Straight away, we ran. But Mum could not keep up, she fell into the eternal abyss.

Hours later, me and Dad were in a crowd of survivors. Hoping, waiting, longing for something good. Will anyone make it through this horrible time, or will we need a new home?

Goodbye for now.

Alastair Brunning (11)
Tunbridge Wells Grammar School for Boys, Tunbridge Wells

The End

Am I alive? I'm dizzy and sick. Everything is gone. My brain is bewildered. I believe, from a memory, that zombies took over.

"Help!" I can see the visions of what happened. I must get rid of this and gallop. I see holes appearing everywhere.

"No!" I have fallen into a peculiar sewer. "Where am I?"

In the distance, I can see a light. What is this? I speculate. I can see loads of katanas. Is this the Ninja Turtle base? Then a door flings open. I rotate around to see the Ninja Turtle squad! They are holding mythic katanas!

Ethan Byrne (12)
Tunbridge Wells Grammar School for Boys, Tunbridge Wells

Mark Man

Fear. Doom. Domination. Purge. Yep! That's me. In a sticky-ish situation. Women shrieking. Children crying. Mark Man to the rescue.

Rifle, bagged. *Bang!* A bomb! I sprint down the staircase of my house. *Pop! Pop!* "Ugh, now I have to clean the carpet!" *Splash!* "What was that noise?"

I take cover but see five armed men. I fire my gun multiple times and they all die. I leave to a silent street.

Could this war be over? Did Mark Man win? Humanity is relieved, and the world is in peace. Mark Man is a true hero.

Mark French
Tunbridge Wells Grammar School for Boys, Tunbridge Wells

Project Armageddon

Then I flipped the switch; smoke filled the room but when it cleared my beast awoke. He stared me down, then sprinted off and into Buckingham Palace. The guards shot it as much as they could but the titanium skin I gave it deflected every bullet that fired at him.

He then rampaged the streets of London; every step was like a miniature earthquake. People fled from the streets and into nuke shelters but only some survived the deadly wrath of my creation.

Then Britain's deadliest weapon came, a laser cannon, but even that could not pierce the indestructible skin.

Charlie Adams (12)

Tunbridge Wells Grammar School for Boys, Tunbridge Wells

Earthquake Rita Destroys Much Of Britain

The ground shook again. The house was falling apart. My step-sister and step-dad had already left for France whilst I was asleep, two days ago. I was trapped in the house. The windows and doors were locked.

The only sign of civilisation was the television. A man was speaking rapidly with an anxious expression plastered on his face. The TV flashed once more, before falling to the floor, shattering the screen. The house was rumbling. There was no haven.

A deafening crack vibrated through the household and the roof gave in. I screamed. The silence of death arrived...

Maxwell Carter (12)

Tunbridge Wells Grammar School for Boys, Tunbridge Wells

World War Three

A grenade flew past my head and landed a few metres behind me. *Bang!* Flames burst into the atmosphere. The chalky thick smoke blurred my vision, everybody was shooting blind. My heartbeat rapidly increased, my legs started to slow and my body shut down. I was scared!
My mind flicked back to when I was on holiday, when I was safe. The sun beamed down on my skin, the sand crunched beneath my feet and the smoke puffed from the barbecue leaving a wonderful aroma behind.
"Get up, run!" My body started like a car engine... "Argh! I am shot!"

Tyus Wiltshire (12)
Tunbridge Wells Grammar School for Boys, Tunbridge Wells

World War III

We were watching TV when it changed to the prime minister. "To all listeners, war has been declared by Russia. Please hide as soon as you hear this announcement!" Sirens resonated as we searched for a hiding place. We resorted to the cabinet under the stairs and crammed inside whilst bombs crashed into London.

After hours of hiding, the bombs were still going off. Many banged on our door, begging for help but we didn't leave our spot. This was until our window smashed. I could hear a foreign language. We covered our mouths as the door creaked open...

Sebastian Jiggins (12)

Tunbridge Wells Grammar School for Boys, Tunbridge Wells

The Woods!

A gust of wind swished and pushed, loosening my only hope of survival in the Alidate. I crept through the woods, the trees unburdened by the moon's rays.

Violent screeches were heard in the distance. The cold was like a sharp dagger poking and slashing my skin.

Not far away from me, I heard a screeching sound. It was quite low but vehement. I was being watched. The trees stood tall and ominous, staring down at me. Gleaming bloodshot eyes stared into my soul. I heard a soft crunch of frosted leaves.

Darkness.

The ambience was as quiet as a tombstone.

Charlie Blaker (12)
Tunbridge Wells Grammar School for Boys, Tunbridge Wells

The Everlasting War

It was official. War had been declared. Russia had invaded Poland; Poland was backed by Europe and America. Russia was backed by Asia and Brazil.

It seemed as though it would be a war quicker than light. It was anything but quick. In fact, it would be an everlasting war; millions would fight in tough, disastrous conditions day after day, year after year, decade after decade. Many soldiers thought that there would be an end to this eternal hellhole. Despite the enlightening thought of the war ending, others knew it wouldn't end. Unless a nuclear bomb was released.

Freddie Gipp (13)
Tunbridge Wells Grammar School for Boys, Tunbridge Wells

How I Killed My School

I was too busy having a splendid time and I forgot what was coming. It was one day until the treacherous living prison with holes everywhere sucking you into a room of solitude, trapped behind metal fences with deadly guards keeping you captured within the bowels of the grounds. School! I called my crew to stop this; today it was going down. We had many ideas, however, we settled on using my dad's truck. We drove the truck into position, dodging the eyes around us, and put a weight on the pedal. It went speeding towards school. We took cover. *Bang!* Oops!

Ethan Tsui (12)
Tunbridge Wells Grammar School for Boys, Tunbridge Wells

The Last Stand

We were alone. Stuck in the deserted wasteland. Surrounded by nothing. Bullets lay next to dead soldiers. Land mines dispersed like ants in an anthill. Death condensed the atmosphere. Everywhere death stood. It was traumatising but they were nearing. Homes were wrecked but the only trace of the major city was the demolished cathedral in the centre, where resources were kept at the start of this tragic war.

As the enemy started closing in, the horrendous nightmare of our demise began to become even more true. As we started to see enemy colours, we felt dead...

Arthur Magoola (13)
Tunbridge Wells Grammar School for Boys, Tunbridge Wells

Solenopsis' Incursion

As the jumping ants left their hanging nest, they were hit with a piercing shock. The bitter, toxic scent of hemolymph, and a wave of plague of smoke and embers. Fire ants. Hordes of stingers and mandibles and the smell of smoke accompanying them. Feared, burning vermillion and scarlet chitin flowed below them like a river of venom; while the jumping ants swarmed the trees, fire ants teeming after them, leaf to leaf. Every jump was a risk, a gamble - leaps from enemies behind put their life in their aim. One slip; one ant dead. Masses of fire ants, swarming everywhere.

George Sillett (12)
Tunbridge Wells Grammar School for Boys, Tunbridge Wells

The Accident

I didn't mean for this to happen. It was all my fault. I was just looking for a space and my brother just tripped around the corner! Mum was going to be heartbroken and I didn't see anyone for help. I needed someone. "Anyone! Please! My brother isn't breathing!" No one could hear me.
I reached into my pocket to grab my phone and call 999. "Help! My brother is senseless. Please, help. I was driving and he turned around the corner without checking! I couldn't brake quick enough to halt! It is all my fault! What should I do now!?"

Billy Allcorn (12)
Tunbridge Wells Grammar School for Boys, Tunbridge Wells

How I Died

It caught alight. Looking back, I realised the Caronia was sinking. Facing the end of my life, I prayed to God. Everything went black.

Five minutes earlier, a Kraken grabbed on. The captain fired his flamethrower to kill, but not it, me. The Caronia caught fire.

All 2,672 people aboard perished. Most of us went to Heaven. My body lies in the North Sea. I'm in Heaven but the captain's in Hell. Remember, you're reading a dead man's story. Edward Smith's story. My story. I had kids and a wife. But water cold as lead made me stone-cold dead.

Harry King (11)
Tunbridge Wells Grammar School for Boys, Tunbridge Wells

The Shadows That Plague My Thoughts

They're back again. The shadows. My eyes snap open; my body is clammy, my sheets are constricting. With a gasp, I throw them off of me.

I creep towards the balcony of my apartment. I open the doors and stare down at the ground, twelve floors below me, and then they are pushing me forward. I stumble away from the shadows, breathing heavily. I feel the rug beneath my heels and look towards my bedroom. Instead, I see the shadows.

The chilling midnight breeze penetrates my threadbare pyjamas. I am pushed towards the balcony, and then I am suddenly falling.

Maren Grover (12)
Tunbridge Wells Grammar School for Boys, Tunbridge Wells

The Carpet Of Death

I walked down the lifeless street that was laced with bodies, like stitches weaving down a blood-red carpet. The air was filled with faint shrieks of desperate fear.

Suddenly, a man leapt out of the alleyway! His arms stretched out towards me. My sword jumped up and swung towards him. A miss!

Calmly, I dived back, avoiding several lunges from him and I readied my weapon. Then I reached forward and sliced the head off the man. Another Infecty slain.

The body fell to the ground, adding yet another stitch to the carpet of death.

When would it end?

Javier Oliver Torrijos (13)
Tunbridge Wells Grammar School for Boys, Tunbridge Wells

The End

Three, two, one. Happy New Year! But wait, there is a large flaming ball. Steven, turn the camera to the flaming ball. As you can see, it's coming towards us. Oh wait, take cover! *Boom!* I can now reveal that there is a large army of fire snakes?! We can definitely reveal that they are fire snakes. Stay on. Stand by. Someone was killed by those vicious snakes. Correction, two people. Correction, I can't count anymore. All I can see is orange flares. Steven look, this chicken's in flames! No! Those irritating swans have killed him. Now just run!

Yuvraj Singh (12)
Tunbridge Wells Grammar School for Boys, Tunbridge Wells

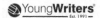
Imminence...

I brushed the ashes off my face. Something terrible had happened. I glanced into the sky and before my eyes was a vast meteor, ripping through the sky, guided by lines of scorching fire.
I trembled and fell to my knees, my whole life there before me. I could feel each water drop sloshing onto my tense cheeks, flowing down like a river.
The crust of the Earth began to crumble and shatter. The meteor was no less than a mile away from the Earth, almost kissing it. The meteor edged closer,
annihilating blocks of cement. Sweet reverence. *Crash!*

Zakarya Haouani (12)

Tunbridge Wells Grammar School for Boys, Tunbridge Wells

The Beast

The earth convulsed and bellowed with the might of a thousand lions. I felt as if I was going to collapse. Everyone across London was shrieking, trying to get to safety. Suddenly, all was quiet. For the first time in days, peace and blissfulness spread over London. However, it didn't last as soon after the ground began to rumble again and erupted with such force and vexation that even the buildings seemed to cower in alarm.
When I looked back at the explosion, all my utmost fears seemed puny compared to the beast staring deep into my petrified soul.

Oscar Du Toit (12)
Tunbridge Wells Grammar School for Boys, Tunbridge Wells

The Stalker

Running, running fast. Shrieks sounded throughout the darkness. They were near. I could feel it. The luminous bolts of lightning were just enough to create me a path through the mangrove. As rain fell around me, a deafening screech echoed, but not like any I had heard before. Five seconds went by until another squeal broke out, but closer than last time.

I dived into some cover but fell into a clearing covered in human-like prints. I could see something in the shadows. A figure, hunched down crying. It turned to face me head on, tears streaming. The Stalker.

Danny Germer (13)
Tunbridge Wells Grammar School for Boys, Tunbridge Wells

The Comet Catastrophe

A bright light appeared, soaring across the sky and a sonic boom was heard. Hours later, news reached that a comet had impacted a nuclear base and so craters were formed in America and in the Pacific Ocean. A tsunami engulfed Hawaii and sea levels rose for many places bordering the Pacific.

The next day, news broke out that all sea levels had decreased and that the Atlantic had got larger. This was because Pacific seawater had filled the crater so the tides changed. This meant the Channel and the Irish Sea got thinner and Europe, Africa and Asia got bigger.

Andrew Macleod (12)
Tunbridge Wells Grammar School for Boys, Tunbridge Wells

The End Of The World

I opened the door to the abandoned facility. I heard a scream, but nothing like a human. The ground started shaking.

A dark, gloomy, eight-foot figure came charging at me. I tried to move but got swatted to the side before I could even blink. I had let something terrible into the world that day.

It was the seventeenth of June 1994, and I watched the evening news. People were aware. Rumours spreading. People were found, hanging from trees. Others turned inside out.

From that day on, I always looked over my shoulder in deep remorse. It was coming.

Olly Brown (14)
Tunbridge Wells Grammar School for Boys, Tunbridge Wells

Untitled

Pedro held his breath. He was underneath his bed, his face pressed up against the cold floor. He could see his mother kneeling, pleading for her life. Seven-year-old Pedro didn't know what was going on. He wished he could be with his mum but she had truly told him to stay quiet and not come out.

A man shouted in a language Pedro didn't know. He could hear quick footsteps getting louder; then two men entered the room. They were carrying pistols. His mum started crying.

A shot sounded. Blood splattered everywhere and his mum fell to the ground.

Albert Edwards (12)
Tunbridge Wells Grammar School for Boys, Tunbridge Wells

Just A Dream

The plane ride was going smoothly. Nothing bad had happened yet.
Suddenly, a massive gust of wind blew the plane off course. The pilot tried to get it back on track, but it was too late! The plane had already hit the side of a mountain. It was rapidly going down quicker and quicker with every second. The plane had crashed in the middle of Antarctica. Out of the one hundred and two passengers that had gotten on the plane, only thirteen survived.
Weeks had passed and all they had eaten was human flesh. Suddenly, Jacob realised, it was all just a dream.

Ruairi Brennan (12)
Tunbridge Wells Grammar School for Boys, Tunbridge Wells

Never Seen Disaster

The waves were retreating like an army under a catastrophic attack. Everyone was running for high ground, but the water was latching onto them and rapidly pulling them under, piercing bodies in an instant. Buildings were sliced like a knife through butter as the waves grew and grew and grew. Everybody was being slaughtered and, one by one, the population shrank until only a few people remained.

But, this minority had just mere minutes to live. A great nuke had been spotted ready to launch itself into the deep waters of what was left of the United Kingdom.

Etienne Saunders (14)
Tunbridge Wells Grammar School for Boys, Tunbridge Wells

The Robots

Out in the open, unprotected, was where I lay. I'd been shot, just like so many others. I heard robotic cheers. *No, it can't be.* London was the only city left. Where should I run?
I bandaged my wound and ran. I ran for days until I saw the ruins of Cornwall. I needed to get to France. If I made it there, I'd survive.
Apparently, the robots malfunctioned and were now harmless. I dived into the ocean and swam. Once I finally made it to shore, I was surrounded. They'd followed me here!
Suddenly, I realised I was dreaming.

Thomas Sweeney (12)
Tunbridge Wells Grammar School for Boys, Tunbridge Wells

The London Invasion

Yesterday, everything changed. The prime minister declared that the Earth was under attack by alien forces. Their ships have blocked out all sunlight, making the night permanent. They hover in the sky snatching up anyone that leaves their home.

I watch them out my bedroom window, starving hungry, deprived of food, wondering why we deserve to suffer. A knock at the door startles me. It is my mum with the only piece of rationed food I'm allowed per day.

Another crash makes my mum drop the food. A tentacle from the ship grabs me. I'm done for.

Alex Stockton (13)

Tunbridge Wells Grammar School for Boys, Tunbridge Wells

The End

Rumble. Bang. Crash. Everything went dark. Debris enveloped me like someone strangling me. I tasted blood. I battled against rubble until I saw light.

I climbed out of the wreckage and looked around. In the blink of an eye, I saw a bullet dart past me. A soldier with a gun ran at me. The Nazis had struck. My first instinct was to run and never stop running. I ran in zigzags, dodging each bullet as the soldier gained. But then I heard it. I heard a bomb ticking away at my feet.

"Goodbye," uttered the soldier. Everything went dark.

Will Steer (12)

Tunbridge Wells Grammar School for Boys, Tunbridge Wells

The Bunker

Dear Diary,
It's been three days since the bomb hit. Who knows what happened to the others? There are only four of us in the bunker, and I don't know how much longer I can take it. One of us left for supplies an hour ago, and he still isn't back. I'm really worried.

Dear Diary,
It's been five days since he left. I think one of the creatures found him.
Collin just died of some illness. I don't know what it is. There are mushrooms all over him. There was a rat in the vents. Wait. A... girl? Wait. Help!

Isaac de Ruiter (11)
Tunbridge Wells Grammar School for Boys, Tunbridge Wells

The Catastrophic Storm

Yesterday, everything changed. Yesterday, England found a small storm coming our way. It looked tiny, not big at all, but that all changed.

It seemed like a gift from hell, meant for death. In the corner of my eyes, I saw cars filled to the brim with corpses from the crash. *How is it still going?* I thought to myself. *If I don't get food, no one can. I am going to die.*

A few days later, half of England was gone, annihilated by the flood. It was a massive catastrophe. What happened on day seven meant death was inevitable.

Lewis Ketterer (12)

Tunbridge Wells Grammar School for Boys, Tunbridge Wells

The Day It Changed

I remember the day well, 22nd February 2022. The day my life changed forever.

It started like any moral day, then the amber alert, but before I could even check it the radio stuttered on. I tried to turn it off. Nothing. Then I tried changing the channel but they were all saying the same thing. "Dan Asenburg, please report to the government offices immediately!"

Bewildered and in shock, I noticed the people driving by all looking at me as if they all knew me and at the same time they didn't. They all knew that I was Dan Asenburg...

Mackenzie Garstang (13)

Tunbridge Wells Grammar School for Boys, Tunbridge Wells

Fire

The thick smoke was choking as fire rained down. I
scrambled down the hill horrified. Where was everyone else?
What had happened? Darkness and fire engulfed the
horizon. In the town nothing moved.
"Hello?" I called. Nothing. Terror mounted. Was I the last?
No, I couldn't be. But it was true. I was the last of my kind.
I sadly watched the fires in the distance slowly die. I had to
find shelter or the fire-breathing monster would kill me too.
As the fires calmed around me I knew it was taking a
breath. It was going to unleash fire.

Will Clarke (13)

Tunbridge Wells Grammar School for Boys, Tunbridge Wells

How Forgetting Things Became Contagious

As me and my friend trudged towards the playground in the sweltering heat, we spotted a water fountain. In our excitement, we ran towards it.

When I pressed the button it released a purple syrup. I grimaced at the thick lilac mixture, but my friend pushed me away and drank it without thinking twice. His face began to go pale and his hand shook when he wrote. I asked him if he was feeling well, but he couldn't tell me. I realised that he couldn't remember how to speak!

This moment was the beginning of the end of everyone's memories.

Szymon Pelczynski (14)
Tunbridge Wells Grammar School for Boys, Tunbridge Wells

Z-Day

The end has come. They have come, the virus began here in London. If you get it, you are gone. Half of the world's population was decimated, and hordes roamed the cities. The virus causes pale skin, glassy eyes and ruptured flesh. On March 20th 2024, the streets ran red with blood. It was a bio-weapon. We didn't know where to go.
I huddled into a ball and prayed for the end. I heard screams cut short. They were here, systematically killing everyone in Britain. My name is Matthew Hardwood, this is my story. I have to warn you. Just run.

Bill Chesworth (12)
Tunbridge Wells Grammar School for Boys, Tunbridge Wells

Shook

Yesterday everything changed. It was meant to be just a normal day in London until it happened. The ground shook beneath my feet. I looked around and sure enough, it wasn't just me who had felt it, everyone was looking around wondering what had happened. The ground shook again. I looked up just in time to notice a small house collapse. I tried to steady myself, but I was still trembling. Panic overtook me. I stood there, paralysed with fear. Screams of panicked citizens filled the air. Sweat trickled down my face. Could this be it? Was this the end?

Hezekiah Cuthbert (11)
Tunbridge Wells Grammar School for Boys, Tunbridge Wells

A Flash Of Fire

With desperation in his eyes, Axel pulled on the joystick but it was a feeble attempt. The flaming helicopter collided with the ground in a dazzling shower of sparks.

His tired eyes flickered open. As he stumbled from the wreckage the engine exploded. His feet left the ground. In a flash of fire, Axel was flung through the air...

As he woke, he glimpsed a blazing orange mass. Axel tried to run but was overcome with pain. He closed his eyes and embraced the brilliant heat of the fire. His body went limp and was lost to the evergrowing inferno.

Xander Lonie (12)

Tunbridge Wells Grammar School for Boys, Tunbridge Wells

The End Of The World

Yesterday, the world changed. It was a normal summer afternoon when over my school building a gigantic black hole suddenly appeared in the pink sky. Monsters and aliens descended from a starship.

I was petrified; the world became dark. In every direction, I heard screams of pain. I ran home to find it was being patrolled by an alien ship and a monster with ten eyes, 100 teeth and a penchant for blood.

Suddenly, the world rumbled; it split in two only five yards away, and magma spilt over our freshly cut grass. Is this the end of the world?

Olly Brooks (12)
Tunbridge Wells Grammar School for Boys, Tunbridge Wells

I Only Meant To Help

I didn't mean for this to happen. I didn't know what I was doing, I only meant to help.

I was running. I didn't know where to, all I knew was that I had to run.

The thick undergrowth I should have been running through had been reduced to ashes. The few trees that were left were peppered with bullets. All the wild animals had died, along with their habitats.

It was apocalyptic.

Suddenly I heard the barking of dogs behind me and that's when I knew, knew that I either had to run or die in the jaws of those monsters.

Oliver Swann (12)

Tunbridge Wells Grammar School for Boys, Tunbridge Wells

The Four Rings

They were right there. I had already stolen the first two rings, but there were lots of enemies and so many I probably couldn't take them on. I was dead, but then I remembered what my father had said, "Do the deed before the problem is made."

So I ran at the colossus monster and the flying beasts above it. My heart was pounding, my arms aching and the rings were getting to strike. I did. Tidal waves swelled the monster and flaming serpents slithered across to the wind beasts and choked them to ashes. The deed was done. Finally...

Leon Williams (12)
Tunbridge Wells Grammar School for Boys, Tunbridge Wells

Devils, Demons, I Don't Know What It Was

The lights flickered on. I walked towards the door and twisted the handle. What awaited me I was not ready for. There was blood up the walls. Guts spread across the floor. Dreading to open the next door and find more of this treacherous smell of death, it creaked as it opened. I saw a creature with an almost circular, squid-like mouth outlined with jagged, flesh-ripping teeth. Then the lights were off and the scuttling was coming closer.
I ran and ran and ran until my breath was gone. I knew the thing was targeting me. Silence. Screams.

Tommy Sands (12)
Tunbridge Wells Grammar School for Boys, Tunbridge Wells

Time Is Little

As I strode through the bustling, lively city, I glanced at my watch, wide eyed. Dodging the bullets of people who were sprawling around, I fixed my eyes on the red finish line, with a tsunami of people storming out of it, and quickened my pace more. Harsh whiffs of petrol wandered towards my nose, but was brutally demolished by the smell of a pastry shop. My bus seemed to move further, yet stayed still, struck by a blaring *honk!* I jumped across the red crossing man. Clock ticking with my heart racing, my interviewer was waiting for me.

Stefan Van Der Merwe (12)
Tunbridge Wells Grammar School for Boys, Tunbridge Wells

The Pavement

I had almost forgotten my book again. I didn't want to get a detention. Finally outside, I checked the time on my phone and headed out to the pavement to tie my laces. I put my phone next to me and crossed the road.

Today was like any other day. I went across the park and up the hill every day at 8. That's where my school was. Anyway, I was now at the park and I saw Hassan's puppy.

Like always, I reached for my phone in my right pocket and... it wasn't there. Left pocket? Not there. Then I remembered... The pavement...

Hassan Elzaafarany (13)

Tunbridge Wells Grammar School for Boys, Tunbridge Wells

Stuck

I was stuck! They'd caught me and now I couldn't escape. Two of them grabbed me and held me against the wall, while another pulled out a gun.

"Please don't kill me!" I said desperately. They ignored my pleading, loaded the gun, aimed it at my head while putting a finger over the trigger and fired. Luckily they missed and it gave me time to escape the two larger men's grasps and run back out of the alleyway they'd caught me in.

I got into their truck and drove away as fast as I could across the wasteland.

Jack Wetz (12)
Tunbridge Wells Grammar School for Boys, Tunbridge Wells

Into The Abyss

I can't believe it! It all happened so fast! One moment I'm digging, next thing I know, my life's almost over. However, I must pull myself together to tell the story. Here we go. Yesterday I was digging a little hole when I noticed a small crack appearing near to me. At first, I thought it was nothing, but then it grew and grew and grew until...
Kaboom! The world split in half! Little did I know this was just an earthquake, but I jumped to the other side. I'd risked the fall but I slowed and fell into the abyss...

Arthur Mountain (11)

Tunbridge Wells Grammar School for Boys, Tunbridge Wells

Morning Mum

I awoke, slamming my alarm and went to check on Mum. She hadn't touched her medication and was nowhere to be found. I heard a creak behind me, then a moan.

It was Mum. Her skin was pale, her skin sagging, her eyes, dead. She lunged at me, smashing an old vase. Shards slit my arm, blood trickled out.

I felt a glass shard on the floor and instinctively stabbed it into the creature. Its wound bled into mine, falling victim to slumber, slumping into bed.

I awoke later, having a hunger needing to be fulfilled, for human flesh.

Sam Saunders (13)
Tunbridge Wells Grammar School for Boys, Tunbridge Wells

The Earthquake

Yesterday my life changed. The ground trembled beneath me as an earthquake ripped across the land with its destructive force. Buildings swayed before collapsing into rubble. Everything went dark and I struggled to breathe amidst the dust and debris. Panic and fear gripped my heart, there was a period of eerie silence before I started hearing cries for help.
I dragged myself out from underneath fallen objects, staggering to stand. I could see the city skyline was completely flattened and I knew nothing would be the same for a long time.

Blake Barlow (11)
Tunbridge Wells Grammar School for Boys, Tunbridge Wells

The Behemoth Of The Thames

Striding on the rock pavement in Picadilly Circus, I felt a rather shocking rumbling beneath the soles of my feet. Something was moving. Destined to find out what it was, I sprinted to the Thames and then I found it. A huge gleaming red eye appeared beneath the glossy surface of the river, and it seemed to be seething with rage.

Traumatised, I called the closest Uber, but nothing was waiting for me at my stop. Unsettling shivers went down my spine. It was me and it.

This is the end of my life as I know it. It's over.

Johnny Verrechia (12)
Tunbridge Wells Grammar School for Boys, Tunbridge Wells

Spine-Chilling Diary Entry

Yesterday, as I was playing on my PS7, everything changed. I took my headphones off to hear the screaming and whirring of jet engines as they whizzed past my window. I was home alone whilst my mum was shopping for food and my dad was at work in London. I was petrified, as I had heard my mum and dad talking about the crazy bombings and fires going on in the world. They said it was catastrophic, but yet I stood up and peered out of the window. A ginormous meteor charged into the city, just a few miles away. *It's here. Run. Hide.*

Shea O'Hagan (11)

Tunbridge Wells Grammar School for Boys, Tunbridge Wells

The Earthquake

It was a cold winter's day and Jeff, a fourteen-year-old, brown-haired boy, was walking home from school.
Jeff was just passing Tesco when suddenly, *bang!*
The sound was deafening and was shortly followed by the screeching and screaming from the unfortunate people, who were at the wrong place at the wrong time.
The ground started to shake. Jeff, unbalanced, fell over. His head collided with the concrete floor. He later woke up in hospital, confused and afraid.
His memory of that day had been totally erased.

Jack Randall (12)
Tunbridge Wells Grammar School for Boys, Tunbridge Wells

The End Has Come

The news flashed, warning me of the outside. Was it only me? I stepped out onto the balcony; the city was in ruins. The aliens scattered around the floor, their large heads pulsing. The sky became black and a green light opened the clouds. Large shapes flew down onto an empty car, ripping it until there was only red dust. In the blink of my dust-filled eyes, they ran into the distance, to the nuclear power plant. *No*, I thought to myself as they devoured the tubes. All of a sudden a ringing and bright light, then, darkness.

Alex McGourty (12)
Tunbridge Wells Grammar School for Boys, Tunbridge Wells

The Shadow

Everything went dark. I was on my own.

Suddenly a ginormous shadow came over me. I panicked as I didn't know what was happening, but then I looked up, my heart racing, my palms sweaty. I closed my eyes almost instantly, not seeing what was there. I could hear breathing. Then my name was being called out. I then realised that they knew me, because they knew my name.

I became less frightened and gathered the strength to open my eyes. When I opened them, I saw my mum screaming at me to wake up because I was late for school.

Jack Bennett (12)
Tunbridge Wells Grammar School for Boys, Tunbridge Wells

Reckless Robots

Dave wandered to the library to get his book. He saw an odd green glow coming from the vent outside the library. He thought nothing of it.

Dave went over to the section about history. He found an unusual-looking book at the back of the shelf. He looked at the title reading 'The Plague'. Since he had not read about the plague, he picked it up. It made a clicking noise.

He fell through the floor and into a hole. He saw blueprints of robots. Distant voices were heard. He looked for a way out.

Green glow! The vent!

Clarke Henry (11)
Tunbridge Wells Grammar School for Boys, Tunbridge Wells

Earthquake

A little boy and his Labrador were strolling around the city when someone started screaming. He didn't know what was going on. Maybe someone had fallen over or burnt themselves... Well, that was what he thought.
Then the ground started to shake. Now he knew what was going on. He had to make a decision, die with the dog or live without it. He loved his dog but he had to leave it.
The boy ran. The dog couldn't, it was too old. Buildings fell, rubble was everywhere, but the boy was safe. The dog didn't make it.

Seth Cockfield (12)
Tunbridge Wells Grammar School for Boys, Tunbridge Wells

Alone

Was I the only one left? There was a murder in my house I think, but I was shivering, hiding under the dark, gloomy bed. Footsteps echoed throughout the corridor as an ominous, hellish laugh made my heart skip a beat. I was terrified and... the ground below me creaked!
Just then the laughter vanished into a deafening silence. The room became a domain of endless darkness...
Suddenly air breathed on my skin. I dared not to look behind. Dread drenched my body. The air around me froze as still as a statue. I knew my fate...

Abdelrahman Elzaafarany (13)

Tunbridge Wells Grammar School for Boys, Tunbridge Wells

Wagamama Nightmare

I visited Wagamama to indulge in a ramen. Everything was well.

As I went to leave, I got a paper cut. I sucked it, it tasted like broth. Odd. My eyes started to tingle. I saw my eyes in a mirror, going green, like an edamame bean. I stumbled down the stairs. Unstable, I grabbed the rail. It transformed into a noodle. I went to fall. I grabbed someone's shoulder. Then they flopped on the floor like a noodle.

Finally, I realised what happened. I am ramen and whatever I touch turns into a noodle. A Wagamama nightmare!

Luca Smith (13)

Tunbridge Wells Grammar School for Boys, Tunbridge Wells

The Volcano

2147, August 21st, lights flickering. I felt a rumbling in the ground, heat flaring. I saw red in the distance. Lava across the world.

I ran to my car. Driving at speeds too high, I reached Gatwick. Carnage. I reached the ticket queue. Time was ticking, I prayed. I sprinted to the first terminal I could find. I ran onto a plane. I was suffocating. We rose and rose, and we reached the centre of the Earth, praying that the water would stop the lava. It was close and like a miracle, it stopped. A new beginning has begun.

Harry Mucklow (12)
Tunbridge Wells Grammar School for Boys, Tunbridge Wells

Parisian Catastrophe

I awoke to a dark room with my hands bound together. I was unable to remember what happened before this. A Russian voice spoke, but I was unable to decipher what he was saying.

My survival instinct then kicked in and I spotted a tinted window. I bolted for it and smashed straight through the glass. It shattered and I fell. My hands cut free.

A voice then bellowed, "Get him!" Halfway down the fall, a blinding light and deafening sound erupted and shockwaved me. All I was able to see was the Eiffel Tower fall.

Lewis Hayter (12)

Tunbridge Wells Grammar School for Boys, Tunbridge Wells

The Zombie Apocalypse

"This is log number 126 on the 9th of December 2036: a zombie outbreak started almost half a year ago. I live in a leftover nuclear bunker. I use it as a shelter from the outbreak. I live with my friend. This is how it started.
It was July in 2036 and a super old grave had been found which contained things never seen before. This included the zombie fluid. They ran tests on it. On July 27th one drank it. He turned into a hideous zombie creature which can infect anyone it touches. And that's how we got here."

Owen Garner (11)
Tunbridge Wells Grammar School for Boys, Tunbridge Wells

The Lost Dog

The house starts shaking, the walls are crumbling. My dog is whining. This can only mean one thing. *Earthquake!* I hear a crack and I sprint outside, terrified. My house collapses. I get out safely but I realise my dog is still inside. Immediately, I start moving the rocks out the way searching for Beau, my dog. Whining, I must be getting close. I spot one of Beau's paws under rocks. I move away the rocks. Beau is injured but alive.

Another rumble happens and rocks fall on Beau and I. Will we escape?

Joseph Johnson (12)
Tunbridge Wells Grammar School for Boys, Tunbridge Wells

Untitled

I woke up to a mind-boggling alarm, which made me groan in anger. I left my bed and did my morning routine, then suddenly, it clicked: my finals were today, and all I did yesterday was play on my Xbox.
In my mind, I thought, *no, no, no! This can't be happening! I'm screwed! Urgh! My mum is going to kill me!*
After realising that there was no way I could pass my finals, I just accepted my fate. The walk to the car felt like years. It was agonising.
Well, here I go.

Pranav Gurram (13)
Tunbridge Wells Grammar School for Boys, Tunbridge Wells

The Power Outage

The lights go off.

"Mum, turn the power on!"

"I can't," she says.

"Ugh!" I sigh. How hard could it be? To my horror, the switch refuses.

Shouting in the distance, "The whole neighbourhood!"

Let me post this on YouTube - 'Wifi and data weird'.

Suddenly, my walkie-talkie speaks. "Stay inside until further notice, power outage across the globe." I start pacing across my bedroom and realise, how will I charge my phone? Nooo!

Dexter Carroll (11)
Tunbridge Wells Grammar School for Boys, Tunbridge Wells

The Death Of Solomon Sallow

I was having the worst day ever. My friend and I, Godric Gaunt, decided to duel my Uncle Solomon. We did this because I thought he was never there for me.

Godric and I were wizards, like my uncle.

Everything went dark after our duel. We were using all advanced spells on Solomon. Until I used dark magic. I used Wingardium Kedavra, the killing curse, on Solomon.

Godric stared at me, startled at Solomon, whose flesh began to fall away until he eventually fell into the clutch of death's hands...

Aditya Kampani (12)

Tunbridge Wells Grammar School for Boys, Tunbridge Wells

Enveloping Flames

On a bright hot summer's day, Sam was enjoying himself in the park playing football. After scoring the final goal, he decided to drop by his grandad Tom's house for a snack. It was a scorching hot day and the route to his grandad's house was on a small track through the woods.
As he strode through the woods, suddenly he became enveloped in smoke. He coughed and spluttered but couldn't see where he was going. In an instant, there were towering flames surrounding him. How could he get out?!

Joel Philpott (12)
Tunbridge Wells Grammar School for Boys, Tunbridge Wells

1974

It was just a regular day. It was going so well. My life was coming together until it happened. It began in class. I was having a great day until I looked outside. The sky went grey. The buildings fell. Everyone started to scream. The walls began to crack. The lights began to flicker. Did I run? Did I scream?
I ran to the door and tried to run to the fire exit, but I was just too late. My eyes shut, and I became unconscious.
Now I'm stuck here not knowing if anyone is still alive here in 1974.

Hudson Holland-Keefe (12)

Tunbridge Wells Grammar School for Boys, Tunbridge Wells

The AI

It all changed yesterday when a nuke dropped in LA; my dad died that day. In turn, I vowed to take the AI down.
The CIA found the leader of the AI's location, the Mellingus. They were in New Europe, the only place where AI is predominant. I went on a flight to New Europe.
When I landed, I was only ten miles away. I suited up in my eco-suit then jumped from building to building to Fao Temule of the Mellingus. He lay there peacefully. I cast my dagger aiming for the throat. I turned him over...

Jygraj Khamba (12)
Tunbridge Wells Grammar School for Boys, Tunbridge Wells

A Burning Mystery

Monday... and as usual it was bland and cloudy in the streets of Outer London. The clock hit eight and Gabriel was up ready for school in his final two weeks of the year.
As he was about to leave, he saw a big cloud of darkness rise into the dull sky. Out of curiosity, he walked a couple of roads down to see the cloud get darker and a smoky smell get stronger. When he found what the cloud was, he just stood there with shock as soot covered the roads with a blazing red fire moving quickly towards him.

Stanley Bonas (13)
Tunbridge Wells Grammar School for Boys, Tunbridge Wells

Stranded

My eyes opened, I was in the plane but we were not flying. We were stranded. I looked to my left and saw my brother covered in bruises with blood trailing down his pale cheeks from his lifeless head. I tried to wake him up but... nothing. I tried to hold back my tears but they rapidly flowed down my face.

Eventually, I stood up and broke out of the hatch. My heart dropped. Endless dunes rolled as far as the eye could see. The sun beat down onto my bloody, aching, bruised body. What was I going to do?

Oliver Barker (13)
Tunbridge Wells Grammar School for Boys, Tunbridge Wells

The Last Percent

This was a really important moment in my life. I was on a call with my soon-to-be boss of my new job, but suddenly I glanced over at the top right-hand corner of my phone and realised I only had one percent left.

Disaster had struck. I couldn't believe it. I paced around my house looking for a charger, but there were none left in sight.

As I entered my bedroom, it caught my eye. I bounded across the room, only to find out that my phone had died. I dropped to my knees, all hope was lost.

James Bennett (12)
Tunbridge Wells Grammar School for Boys, Tunbridge Wells

Lost And Found

A man was walking in the streets then it all went dark. The ground started to rumble. The man and his dog ran to find shelter but before he got there, he realised his dog was no longer by his side.

Once the earthquake had finally stopped, he went out searching. He asked people whether they had seen him but they all denied it. The man saw a dog that looked identical to his, just way smaller. He followed the dog through to an alleyway where his dog and another lay together surrounded by puppies.

Stanley Grayland (12)

Tunbridge Wells Grammar School for Boys, Tunbridge Wells

The Beginning

"Breaking news, the bomb has been dropped!"
Bang! The lights went out. Gas covered the dead sky. Fires
spread, and ear drums cracked. London turned to ash. Faint
distant screams. Nothing but scratches.
"Retalliate!"
Bombs fired. All I heard were distant murmurs. I lay still, as
more bombs were shot.
I got up, covered in dust and ash. Everything was destroyed.
I looked up. There was mere light, except this bright beam.
That's when it all began...

Daniel Soanes (12)
Tunbridge Wells Grammar School for Boys, Tunbridge Wells

Work Day

I was having the worst day ever; the traffic was bad and it seemed as if all the traffic lights were faulty. At the time, I was listening to the radio to get me through the day when I heard that there was a report of a rogue AI that had become self aware and was trying to cause chaos. Suddenly, I heard an explosion as the building to my right disintegrated. As if the day couldn't get any worse, there was a large metallic figure standing over us. The AI had a body and now it could take control.

Toby Portlock (13)
Tunbridge Wells Grammar School for Boys, Tunbridge Wells

Nuclear Disaster

Crack! I feel a draft of warm air and spot a ladder. I climb down, my arm sweaty. As I reach the bottom, I see a massive drill going down to lava level. I feel thick draughts of boiling air and look down as the lava spews and bubbles. I feel very concerned as to who made this place and why. As I look around the dark area and realise this is why there are cracks in the road, because of the drilling, I look right and see rows of nuclear bombs with a timer unknown. We need to evacuate!

Balthazar Gyring-Nielsen (12)
Tunbridge Wells Grammar School for Boys, Tunbridge Wells

Asteroid

Boom! That was the sound of the asteroid hitting Earth like two boxers in the ring. A devastating ring in my ear as I dusted myself off. We were expecting this to happen but thought NASA would do something to prevent it.

I got myself out of the rubble of what had been my home for the last ten years to see if I could find my family (my parents, a cat and a dog). But they were nowhere to be seen. I shouted their names. No answer.

I was truly alone. No family, no food or water.

Dylan Gregan-Salvado (12)
Tunbridge Wells Grammar School for Boys, Tunbridge Wells

Critical

He was dead; I was the only one left, shivering, weeping and fighting for my life. The bullet stuck deep inside my thigh felt like it was pushing the blood out of my leg on its own. I had to think quickly, it was a matter of seconds before I would be nothing more than a lifeless blob on the cold, hard floor. My eyes darted across the room looking for something that could cover up my wound and stop it from bleeding.
At this point I was about to give in to my fate, but then...

Sebastian Higham (12)
Tunbridge Wells Grammar School for Boys, Tunbridge Wells

The Gash

When I woke up one day, I heard on the news that we should tightly close all windows and blinds. My cat was shouting behind me for food and I almost fed him when I heard that animals were being infected by a new plague that made them violent. I did wake up to scratches on my body. I thought it was just his tendencies. He was still shrieking his head off behind me.

The TV was on a new story about a parrot who could sing. I felt my leg split. I awoke to his form above me.

Andrew Champkin (14)

Tunbridge Wells Grammar School for Boys, Tunbridge Wells

Nuclear Decimation

21st April, 1961, we were ordered into our bunker, conscious of the events that would unfold above us as we dived below. *Screech*. *Rumble*. A door opened revealing our home for the next forty-five years. Despite being as dystopian and hopeless as it may sound, the bunker was fully stocked and state of the art. The heavy door closed.

Then a scream was heard. A loud boom. Everything went black and I collapsed, taking my last breath on this planet.

Nikita Hubin (12)
Tunbridge Wells Grammar School for Boys, Tunbridge Wells

Running Away Forever

During class, the fire bell rang. We exited the door. I panicked. I thought the school would blow up. The fire bell hadn't ever gone off.

Mr Tango came and told us that it was a real fire. This panicked me even more. When we exited through the gates, I took my chance and ran away. I didn't know my way back home, so I turned in to this colourful-looking street. I kept walking down the street. It seemed to become darker and darker and then...

Younus Baig (12)
Tunbridge Wells Grammar School for Boys, Tunbridge Wells

The Air Show Catastrophe

As I woke up I realised I was alive! Then I saw the news and remembered. I touched down on the runway at Paris Air Show then all the lights and alarms came on. I lost control as the plane bounced multiple times. Then to everyone's horror, the plane made one last bounce, then rolled and smashed into the spectator area at one hundred miles per hour.

That was the last thing over five hundred people saw. Then they announced we had been sabotaged!

Theo Slade (12)

Tunbridge Wells Grammar School for Boys, Tunbridge Wells

Fortnite Phone Call

Today was horrid. I was mid-call with my mates before...
Bam! My phone died. I tried to play it out but I couldn't
communicate to my teammates before I was killed. My
mates were killed after. Unfortunately, they kicked me from
the squad.

I went to charge my phone. I thought about how I lived and
chose to finally go outside to touch grass. This was life-
changing.

John Davies (12)
Tunbridge Wells Grammar School for Boys, Tunbridge Wells

The Tsunami

As I was on the beach, enjoying life, square waves appeared in the ocean. At the sight of this, I instantly packed my things and left. A sign of a tsunami.
Instantly I tried to drive out of the city, but as I was on the highway, my car broke down.

James Wong (12)
Tunbridge Wells Grammar School for Boys, Tunbridge Wells

YoungWriters® Est. 1991

YOUNG WRITERS INFORMATION

We hope you have enjoyed reading this book – and that you will continue to in the coming years.

If you're a young writer who enjoys reading and creative writing, or the parent of an enthusiastic poet or story writer, do visit our website **www.youngwriters.co.uk**. Here you will find free competitions, workshops and games, as well as recommended reads, a poetry glossary and our blog.

If you would like to order further copies of this book, or any of our other titles, then please give us a call or visit **www.youngwriters.co.uk**.

Young Writers
Remus House
Coltsfoot Drive
Peterborough
PE2 9BF
(01733) 890066
info@youngwriters.co.uk

Join in the conversation!

 YoungWritersUK   YoungWritersCW
 youngwriterscw   youngwriterscw